Don't Be A DOUCHEBAG

A Man's Guide to Etiquette

"Never underestimate the stupidity of society." – MATTHEW JAMES

A **bundled** eBook edition is available
with the purchase of this print book.

CLEARLY PRINT YOUR NAME ABOVE IN UPPER CASE

Instructions to claim your eBook edition:
1. Download the BitLit app for Android or iOS
2. Write your name in **UPPER CASE** above
3. Use the BitLit app to submit a photo
4. Download your eBook to any device

Engage Books
Mailing address
PO BOX 4608
Main Station Terminal
349 West Georgia Street
Vancouver, BC
Canada, V6B 4A1

www.engagebooks.ca

Don't be a Douchebag
Copyright © 2016 Matthew James
Design © 2016 Engage Books Limited

Designed by: A.R. Roumanis
Cover photo by: A.R. Roumanis.

FIRST EDITION / FIRST PRINTING

LIBRARY AND ARCHIVES CANADA CATALOGUING IN PUBLICATION

James, Matthew, 1982–, author
    Don't be a douchebag : a man's guide to etiquette / Matthew James.

    Issued in print and electronic formats.
    ISBN 978-1-77226-004-5 (bound) –
    ISBN 978-1-77226-003-8 (pbk.) –
    ISBN 978-1-77226-007-6 (pdf) –
    ISBN 978-1-77226-005-2 (epub) –
    ISBN 978-1-77226-006-9 (kindle)

    I. Etiquette for men – Humor.
    I. Title.

PS8619.A64D65 2016   C818'.602
C2014-906053-X
C2014-906054-8

Matthew James

Don't Be A DOUCHEBAG
A Man's Guide to Etiquette

VANCOUVER:
ENGAGE BOOKS LIMITED
2016

This book is dedicated
to real men the world over.
I'm talking about all you hairy chested,
five o'clock shadowed,
beer guzzling hooligans out there.
This is your book,
dammit!

CONTENTS

INTRODUCTION

WHEN I SAT DOWN to write this book, I had but one thought in mind: I wanted to change the world. Mission accomplished!

This literary masterpiece is exactly what the world has been waiting for, whether the world knows it or not. You must have done something right in your past life to have been granted the good fortune of finding this book in your hands. My witty and genius prose fills the following pages with stories, guidelines and rants that will enlighten and enrich your life. You're welcome!

I have written the ultimate man's guide to living. Let this book be your bible. Well, not the *bible* bible. I'm not so high on myself that I'd compare my writing to the writings of the Lord. I wouldn't want anyone to think that I have created some sort of religious scripture or anything like that. But, if someone were to create a cult based on my writings, that would be alright, I supposed. That is as long as I can be the guy at the top of the pyramid collecting all the membership dues. We could be like the Scientologists, except a little less crazy and demented.

I'm getting side-tracked here so let me get back to the point. This book is going to make you laugh your ass off, literally. My publisher debated categorizing this book as a weight loss tool because many of the chubby people in the focus group laughed the pounds away as they read. That's how funny it is. But more importantly, this book will educate. It will not only illustrate what a douchebag truly is, but it will teach you how to not become one yourself. This is achievable by being the complete opposite of the people I write about. So let me, Matthew James, be your guide on the journey to becoming a truly awesome man. And if you happen to be a lady reader, just sit back and enjoy the ride. You're going to love it! Well, I'm at least forty percent sure you won't absolutely hate it.

50 SURE SIGNS YOU'RE A DOUCHEBAG

1   You always wear a loose fitting muscle shirt that exposes one or both nipples. It may also be emblazoned with a beer logo, mustard and/or motor oil stains and nasty yellow armpit stains.

2   You have a dog that spends its entire existence chained up in your backyard. I hope that Karma catches up to you one day, and by Karma, I mean a big, hairy S&M practitioner named Karma, who will chain you up himself and make you feel like the filthy animal you are.

3   You sport a permed mullet. Not because you lost a bet with your buddies, but because that's who you are.

4   You wear dainty, powder-puff, cream-coloured cashmere sweaters tied around your neck and shoulders. That preppy fool from 80's date movies called. He wants his look back.

5   You have nine children with eight different women.

6   You are a massive nerd but try your hardest to act like you are super cool.

7   You are an awful driver, yet day after day you remain on the road behind the wheel of your vehicle, leaving nothing but gridlock, chaos and near-fatal accidents in your wake.

8   You are the jaywalker who does not look both ways, one way, or any way before crossing the street. Natural selection is calling.

9   You wear nothing but deep v-neck t-shirts and skinny jeans that are hemmed too short.

10   You call everyone 'bro' but pronounce it 'bra.'

11   You are a purse-snatcher, the ultimate coward and a skid mark in society's underpants.

12   You are a lazy traffic cop. Wipe that confectioners' sugar and jelly filling off your shirt and do us all a favour and ram that radar gun right up your clenched sphincter.

13   You are a billionaire CEO, yet the billions that you already have still aren't enough to make you happy. You stop at nothing and perform any type of evil and underhanded deeds to grow your already obscene wealth. Too bad money can't re-grow your hair.

14   You don't piss into the urinal but instead piss on the floor in front of it. Maybe your penis is far too small to aim with? Maybe you are a woman in transition? Either way, sit your ass down on the toilet.

15   You are a filthy rich banker. Bankers are nothing more than pawnbrokers with manicures whose pretty little fingers contribute nothing to society.

16   You are an immigrant who outright refuses to learn the language of your new home country.

17   You smoke in no smoking areas.

18   You are a beer league professional. You take each and every game far too seriously and are willing to injure and maim just to win a 'friendly' game played by middle-aged men on Thursday nights.

19   You own Ticketmaster. A twenty dollar surcharge is highway rob-
     bery. And why do I have to pay extra to print my own tickets on my
     own printer?

20   You are a terrible parent who, among other things, allows his children
     to run rampant like demented wild animals while out in public.

21   You write parking tickets for a living.

22   You stand waiting for elevators right in front of the doors. The in-
     stant the doors open, you push your way in before anybody has a
     chance to walk out. I didn't know they still performed lobotomies.

23   You have a vehicle that is covered with bumper stickers. The num-
     ber of bumper stickers on your vehicle is directly proportional to
     how large of a douchebag you are. That's science.

24   You make 'air quotes' with your fingers in almost every sentence
     you speak.

25   You are a grown man that regularly watches MTV. You are your
     own worst enemy.

26   You wear your pants below your ass.

27   You speak excessively loud while on your cell phone.

28   You wear a baseball hat with a perfectly straight brim.

29   You wear sunglasses at all times, no matter where you are, no matter
     what you're doing, and no matter if it's day or night.

30   You exclusively refer to yourself in the third person. Matthew James
     hates this behaviour.

31 You live in the downtown core of a major city, yet you drive a Hummer. FYI, those little baggies of cocaine in your glove compartment would also fit into an inconspicuous and much smaller vehicle.

32 You wear gallons of cologne. It's like you bath in the stuff. You're a human bomb of teargas.

33 You are a genuine, full-blown racist.

34 You are a hippie. Your outright refusal to bathe, cut your hair, get a job or wear normal clothing are just the tip of the iceberg of what makes you a douchebag.

35 You are a greaseball with an uncanny ability to make women's skin crawl.

36 You are a colossal freeloader. Your wallet suffers from agoraphobia.

37 You are a chronic name-dropper.

38 You are a white man who doesn't know it.

39 You have a lot of money and advertise it the best you can.

40 You are an unpaid critic who posts endless nonsense to the internet.

41 You have a wine-tasting room in your house.

42 You call all movies *films*, without exception.

43 You are an angry sports snob who thinks you know everything there is to know about every sport on the planet yet you are barely coordinated enough to tie your shoes.

44 You are pompous and pretentious and, hey, you think you're better than me, don't you?

45 You exclusively wear nothing for a shirt but a wife beater that is about two sizes too small for you.

46 You crank the volume of your headphones to maximum and wear them hanging around your neck.

47 You refuse to shower for what smells like weeks before you get onto a crowded plane, train, or bus.

48 You are a conscienceless defence attorney. I should have just said you are a defence attorney.

49 You find this book to be offensive.

50 You are reading this book right now but you didn't buy it. No free reads. Buy your own copy and clear your name.

CHAPTER 1

IT'S AN EPIDEMIC

THE WORLD IS FULL of douchebags. That's a fact. It has been scientifically proven and you just can't argue with science. Trust me, I've tried and it's gotten me nowhere - although, it has gotten many a Republican into office.

I figured if I can't beat science, I might as well join it. I, therefore, decided to take a scientific approach to this chapter. What I wanted to explore was if society has always been full of selfish douchebags or if this phenomenon is something that began in the modern world.

So I decided to take to the streets to conduct my research. I spent many gruelling hours in such establishments as pubs, bars, restaurants and even gyms, from time to time. I also hit up some leading university professors who research the subject of douchebagology to examine their findings.

If you believe a word of what I have just written then I should also let you know that as an accidental by-product of my research, I made a new scientific discovery that is going to revolutionize the world of personal lubricants. But that's a story for another day.

The Numbers Have Been Crunched, But I'm Still Hungry

AFTER MONTHS of intense research and scrutiny, pie charts and power-point presentations, I came to the conclusion that there is a douchebag epidemic plaguing our planet today. The douchebag to non-douchebag ratio has grown exponentially over the past fifty years, with nearly five times more douchebags found on the streets today. If you find that hard to believe it's ok, because at first I didn't believe it myself. That was until I saw the pie charts and as we all know pie charts are impossible to manipulate.

Fifty some odd years ago, hippie-ism was in its infancy. Hippies were growing their hair long, refusing to shower or to show up to work and were basically mooching off of society.

Hippies are the original douchebags. I believe they are personally responsible for starting the douchebag revolution. They made it seem cool, among certain circles at least, to be a douchebag. That's not cool!

The hippies' extreme opposition to such things as personal hygiene, complete thoughts and sentences, haircuts and stable employment are what made them pioneers in the field. While douchebags can be found in all aspects of society today, I believe they got their roots back in the days of free love, man.

Over the years, douchebags have branched out as wide as a Mormon's family tree. They have infiltrated themselves into all walks of life and can be found almost anywhere you may roam. It must be some sort of genetic mutation in their brains that makes them the way they are. As far as I can tell, douchebags were put on Earth just to creep out ladies, take up space and piss people off.

Reality My Ass

A DOUCHEBAG is like a virus. He can spread his influence like a flu bug in a sneeze from one moron to the next. This specimen can influence unintelligent people and convince them that it is cool to be a douche-bag. Thus, the virus spreads. And at no time in history has this been more evident than in the past dozen or so years, ever since reality television's massive explosion in popularity.

They are all over television. Douchebags run rampant on all forms of reality TV shows. It's sad and unfortunate, but much of society is drawn to them. Young, dumb and easily impressionable children and teenagers are influenced by these fools, often opting to act and dress like the retards they see glorified every day on TV.

Perhaps the best way to try and decrease the growing douchebag epidemic on this planet is to stop watching mind-numbingly awful reality television shows that, amazingly enough, glorify them. We have to kill the douchebag virus in order to eradicate it. Unfortunately it's a virus that we can't kill with copious amounts of hand sanitizer.

If you want to be a real man, and not a magnificent douchebag, you've got to watch the same television shows that real men watch. Real men play sports and real men watch sports. Real men do not get fake tans, wax their skin baby-smooth, worry about caloric intake, live off their daddy's trust funds and watch television shows about men who do the same.

So man up, grow a sack, sprout some fur on it and help put an end to the viral spread of douchebag behaviour the world over. Stop watching those garbage 'reality' TV shows and the television studios will have no choice but to stop airing them. The only way to make them disappear is to crush their ratings. Society is counting on you. Don't let it down.

CHAPTER 2

WHERE ARE ALL THE REAL MEN GOING?

I TOOK A TRIP to New York City with my wife a few years back. It was a great trip. There's a lot to do and a lot to eat there, and Lord knows I love my food. There were so many great restaurants it made me wish that my stomach was ten times its actual size. But then I would have needed my wallet to have been ten times its actual size as well, because dammit, that city is expensive.

It was my first time in New York, and with it came several new experiences. For instance, I had never before seen so many people crammed into such a small area. Also, I had never before been called a nigger.

The most likely reason for the latter is because I'm a white man. None the less, I was verbally assaulted on a crowded street by a skinny, cracked-out low-life who, in what I can only assume was a drug-induced psychotic rage, threw racist comments at me - a man to which those particular comments were not at all racist and held no meaning. If anything it was comical, especially considering that this wonderfully awful man was himself, black.

The situation all began when my wife and I were taking in the scenery as we walked down the street. The douchebag crack-head had cut right in front of my wife, with whom I was walking hand in hand. He did so while dragging his hoody behind him on the sidewalk like Linus does his blankie.

He cut so close in front of her that she unknowingly stepped on his hoody while she was looking up at a building across the street. It nearly caused her to trip to the ground. Had it not been for me holding her hand, she would have been a goner. Ok, that may be an overreaction. But she certainly would have received a minor abrasion from an impact with the sidewalk.

As she recovered and got her feet back firmly underneath her, the crack-head whipped around in a flash and got right into her face. He then proceeded to call her all sorts of un-gentlemanly things. A moment later, an angry Matthew James had confronted this ill-mannered man and that was when he shifted his verbal assault in my direction, spewing offensive words and names including the aforementioned that really caught me off guard.

But as he was yelling at me, as he got more and more amped up and exaggerated in his behaviour, he had yet to make eye-contact with me. I was giving the look so I obviously couldn't see it, but what it basically expressed was that if he didn't get out of my way that instant, I was going to rip his heart out of his chest and ram it up his rectum until it popped his eyeballs out. Either that or poke him in the eyeball.

The degenerate backed himself up to a safe distance and put about twenty feet between us, the whole while yelling profanities at me and my wife while we remained silent and shocked.

I didn't say anything and I wasn't about to do anything now that he had put such a great distance between us. In doing so, the fool now presented absolutely no harm. He was clearly only interested in putting on a show for the crowd. He did not actually want to have anything to do with me in a scrap. If someone actually wants to fight you, they won't back twenty feet away before picking the fight.

As much as I wanted to cave the douchebag's face in, it was all for the better that he had backed away. I really didn't want to mix it up with this guy, because he would probably have given me hepatitis or AIDS or something like that when he bled on me. I also didn't want to end up in the police station on my vacation, explaining to the NYPD how Crackie McCrack ended up dead at my feet.

After a few more moments of maniacal shouting from one of New York's finest citizens, I got the feeling that the pathetic addict had forgotten exactly who it was that he was yelling at to begin with. Never-the-less, the douchebag wouldn't stop hollering, so the two of us just turned and walked away. As soon as we did, he immediately ceased his delusional tirade and took off. Welcome to New York, Matt and wife.

Dude Looks Like a Lady

ANOTHER NEW experience for me in New York City was witnessing the abundance of men who carried purses. When did this happen?

I know there are a lot of people out there who get enraged every time anyone suggests that there is a difference between men and women, but many of the differences are pretty hard to ignore. My apologies to all the chemically imbalanced, misguided crusaders of gender equality out there, but if I wrote about all the differences between me and my wife alone, you'd be reading well into the night.

Now, I know men have always carried briefcases or backpacks when needed, but not purses. Briefcases are plain and boxy, awkward to carry and utilitarian, just like men. Backpacks come in all different shapes and sizes, also like men - except for the ones covered in pink shag or princess pictures. Purses, on the other hand, are for ladies. They're fancy, expensive, sometime impractical and pretty, just like women.

The thing that gets me is that these man-purses aren't even distinguishable from lady purses. As far as I can tell, they are merely lady purses that are being carried, instead, by men.

Why does a man need a purse anyway? How much stuff does a man actually need to carry with him when he goes out?

Women carry purses because they take half their homes with them every time they go out. In it they usually have a massive wallet - one about three or four times the size of a man's - to hold the mind boggling number of cards that women seem to collect from each and every store they've ever been to. They've also got makeup, tampons, hand creams, hand sanitizers, lip balm, lip stick, tissues and Lord knows what else all crammed into their purses. They basically have a mobile bathroom, bank and convenience store slung over their shoulders everywhere they go.

When I leave the house, all I take with me is a small wallet, a phone and keys. That's it. Everything I take with me can easily fit into my pockets.

Although, I do hate carrying things in my pockets so I do like to unload my stuff into my wife's purse whenever possible. But that's what she's there for. There's no way in hell I would ever carry my own purse. I don't need that cumbersome thing over my shoulder just to carry the small amount of stuff I take with me. Oh, and I'm not a woman. So if my wife's not with me, then my pockets do just fine. I've got to say though, purses do come in handy when trying to sneak booze into theatres or sporting events. I mean, nine bucks for a cup of beer is just ridiculous!

Aside from sneaking large amounts of booze around, why do these girly-men need to carry purses? What could they possibly have crammed into them? Have they become so feminine that they now have a need for maxi-pads and makeup? Do they get periods? I don't get it.

And it wasn't like it was just in one small section of the city that I witnessed this unmanly behaviour either. It was all over! Purse-men were anywhere and everywhere I went. Many of them appeared to be with girlfriends or wives, so I certain, to a degree, that many of them weren't gay. That perplexed me even further.

I mean, why would a straight man want to put out a gay vibe? And why would any man want to look like a woman? I couldn't understand it. I couldn't contemplate why there were so many men in that city that did everything they could to make themselves as feminine as possible. Maybe I'm just too narrow-minded and old fashioned? Nope, couldn't be that.

All this behaviour got me thinking: what's wrong with being a man? I love being a man. I've got muscles on my bones. I've got hair on my chest. I pack a penis with me wherever I go and I never say no to a beer. I have done stupid and irresponsible things to try to impress women, and after a few drinks I think I'm Superman. I don't want to eat lettuce and bean sprouts until all my muscles fade away and I don't want to wear makeup and carry a purse and watch chick flicks while curled up on the couch with a box of tissues. I want to eat thick, juicy steaks and chase them down with copious amounts of beer while I watch football.

I was in a Coach store with my wife after our trip to New York, and I got into a conversation with the two women working there about, of all things, football. For those of you men who do not know what Coach is, as I once didn't (oh how naive and happy I once was), it's a brand of over-priced purses. The store I was in was in Seattle and both women who worked in the store were big Seahawks football fans, as am I.

Anyway, I ended up having a pretty good conversation about the pre-season with the store clerks while my lovely wife browsed the store's contents, quite thoroughly I might add. Eventually, this conversation segued into one of the women telling me that there was now a men's only Coach Store. So I asked her what kind of stuff they sold in the men's store. I wanted to know if it was like the store in which I currently stood or if they sold different merchandise, merchandise for men. The woman told me that it was pretty much the same store - a purse store - but for men.

I started to laugh because I thought she was joking, until she told me she wasn't. I couldn't believe it. I was still coming to terms with the fact that such a ridiculous store would exist for men, when the woman told me that the men's only store was in fact doing so well that they were going to open a second one. Pow! That one staggered me. I didn't see that coming. The apocalypse must be nigh.

Just so you know where I'm coming from, I grew up admiring manly men in a city full of them. I grew up in a mill and lumber town. The only time I ever saw a man with a purse was when he was holding it for his wife as she went to the bathroom.

And even that was a stretch for some men. Some guys would just outright refuse to hold their lady's purses for even a second for fear of being seen by other men. Now, I'm not that crazy or insecure. I've got no problem holding a purse for a lady, but you'll never catch me shopping for my own purse to accessorize my outfit (I just threw up in my mouth a little bit there).

I can more easily come to terms with a gay man carrying a purse than a straight man, because some gay men are girly and feminine - although, there are some pretty rough and tough gay dudes out there too (so don't accuse me of stereotyping, you politically correct wackos). But a supposed straight man with a purse on his shoulder is downright perplexing. Whatever happened to men wanting to be manly?

Since I am not gay I'm going to have to go on assumption here, but wouldn't even gay men find it strange to witness 'straight' men walking around the streets with purses slung over their shoulders?

And it's not always just purses. Many of these dudes had done plenty of other unmanly things as well, such as sculpting their eyebrows and sporting feminine clothes.

Some of these purse-clad men had beards on their faces that must have taken them hours to shave with intricate little designs and shapes carved into them. Many of these weirdoes also had fake tans and I'm pretty sure I saw the odd guy with some makeup on his face. Why don't you just sign up for that sex-change operation already? Trans-anything is pretty hip right now. Go nuts!

No real man, gay or straight, would ever put that much time, effort or consideration into his appearance. For a special occasion I will shave (and by shave I mean my face only…ok maybe my back), shower, put a little gel in my hair and put on some nice clothes. The whole procedure takes thirty minutes, tops. These purse-carrying dudes probably take hours to get ready to go anywhere, even to the supermarket.

Like I said before, this behaviour must even bother gay dudes. I'm sure they're confused as to who to hit on and who to leave be. I mean, it used to be pretty obvious with regards to who was gay and who wasn't, or at least I thought it was (like usual, I'm probably offending some people here). You could walk into a bar and for a large part be like, 'Okay, that guy's gay. He's wearing makeup and holding a purse. But the guy standing next to him with the fashion sense of a retarded hillbilly can't possibly be gay. No gay man would be caught dead wearing that hideous shit.' Maybe I'm exaggerating about it being that cut and dry - because not all gay men are advertising it loud and proud like a walking billboard - and not all straight men are burly lumberjacks (that actually sounds kind of gay too). But these days, especially in a city like New York, it is far from cut and dry when trying to judge a man by his clothing and appearance. That doesn't work well for a stereotyping SOB like me.

I feel like I'm living in a world that's gone mad. Men are trying to be ladies. It's all messed up. I'm so confused right now. I need a beer.

If you're a man that carries a purse, please go find your little man-purse right now and throw it in the trash. And don't just place it in the trash, throw it in there with emphasis. Slam dunk that leather, bitch! Maybe that action will get the testosterone flowing through your veins once again. It will feel good to do something manly for a change, trust me.

If you're not willing to do that though, if you're not willing to perform even one masculine act, then put this book down right now because you're not fooling anybody. You don't need to read a man's guide to etiquette. Stop pretending to be something that you're not and go get the copy of *Little Women* that you keep hidden under your mattress. The charade's over.

Just to make myself clear, if you're gay, have at it. I'm no bigot. I mean, even though his music is probably meant for people much younger than me, I've got no problem with Justin Bieber. And I love Tom Cruise movies. And you don't see either of those dudes walking around with purses, do you?

CHAPTER 3

DISCIPLINE IS EXTINCT

THE PENDULUM of society has really swung hard away from anything resembling discipline, especially over the past couple of decades. Now, don't get me wrong. I'm not a serious prick that likes to suck the fun out of everything. I'm actually more or less a grown man-child. But there are certain times in life that call for discipline, certain instances that call for someone to step up and take charge and nip strange behaviour in the bud.

There are so many little shits running around all over the place that have never heard the word 'No' once in their short little lives (I sound like a ranting old man, don't I?). Not to mention the revolving door of the justice system that gives criminals more rights than it gives victims, essentially re-victimising victims over and over again - much like how The Bachelor keeps returning to TV season after season giving my wife the ammunition to re-victimize me.

What Is This Word 'No' You Speak Of?

WHO RULES THE ROOST: a man, his wife, or their two-year-old little demon-spawn of a child? Well, it seems to me that in many families out there, it's the little shits that run the show.

Whatever Satan's little servant says, goes, and if not, he just throws a tantrum until his pathetically weak parents give up and cave to his will. Whatever mummy and daddy had originally said or wanted goes straight out the window if little Junior disagrees with them and decides to throw a fit.

Many of these moronic parents pride themselves on a ridiculously idiotic principle of never disciplining their children or saying 'No' to them. Some of these parents may have hated how they were raised by their own overly strict parents, and as a result have decided the best course of action for parenting their own children would be to swing in the completely opposite direction and remove all forms of discipline.

These parents somehow think that by not setting any boundaries or limitations for their children, by never letting their kids hear the word 'No' once in their lives, that they will miraculously raise wonderful, well-adjusted children that will become outstanding adult members of society. Keep dreaming! Instead you're raising a child destined for many a playground beat-down.

Your job as a parent is to set an example and to show your kids how to behave in real life. A fucking two-year-old isn't going to be able to figure all that shit out on his own, and if you think he can, it's a shame you weren't born sterile.

I have a two year old son and I feel like I'm doing everything wrong most of the time. My kid will throw temper tantrums at home about absolutely nothing, like me using the wrong type of tissue paper to wipe his nose – I wish I was joking. Some days I feel like he is trying to push me over the edge that I straddle on a daily basis, the edge of my mental sanity. But regardless of any of that, I tell my kid 'no.' I tell him 'No' all the time. And that is because I am a man and he is a child and he will want, or ask for, or do some pretty fucked up shit, and it is my job as the older and wiser one to tell him 'no.' I do not cave to his every will. It's just not in me.

By re-enforcing bad behaviour in kids through never correcting unwanted or inappropriate behaviours, the little ones learn from an early age that they can do whatever the hell they want. If they are ever met with opposition, they fight, scream and holler until they get their way. And because these children have useless pussies for parents, they always get their way. Whenever you see a fifty pound three year old it's because his parents are weak, weak people. They'd rather have a fatty with type two diabetes than have to utter the word 'no.'

By teaching kids that negative behaviour is met with absolutely no consequence, you are setting them up for future failure in life. If you grow up thinking that you can do whatever the hell you want to do whenever the hell you want to do it, you are not likely to become a decent and productive member of society. You will, instead, be more likely to become an inmate. And when Big Leroy has you down on your knees in the shower room, you'll be at a loss because no one ever taught you the word 'No'. If you've never before heard it, how would you know what it means or how to use it? Good news for Leroy, bad news for your sphincter.

Imagine this: little Jimmy is raised by two pathetic parents that, when met by any resistance at all from little Jimmy, fold to his will. Little Jimmy learns from an early age that he can do anything he pleases and if he is ever told otherwise, he simply throws a temper tantrum until he gets his way. He always gets his way. Temper tantrums rock!

One day, when Jimmy is a little older and still regularly throws raging tantrums, he's shopping at a jewellery store and sees a watch that he wants. He tries it on, likes it, and decides to leave the store without paying.

When a store employee follows him out and demands that he pay for the watch, he tells the salesman to piss off. Security is called and Jimmy is apprehended and held until the police arrive. While being arrested, Jimmy (who is no longer so little) throws a temper tantrum, violently throws himself to the floor and resists the police officers. But does the behaviour that has been working for him his entire life work for him now? To his stunning surprise, it does not.

What it does do for him, however, is get him pepper-sprayed and beaten into submission. It also gets him an additional charge added to his charge of theft: the charge of resisting arrest.

The problem is that everyone needs boundaries. If you're never taught right from wrong, and never get an ass-whooping when you step too far out of line, well, then why would you ever toe the line?

Now, that's not necessarily a good analogy because I don't often like to toe the line. But I also don't like to do shit that harms others or steal from stores. And part of the reasoning behind that is the knowledge that if I perform certain acts and get caught in the process, I will go to prison. And a man like me would not fare well in prison. I am incredibly handsome and I'm not the biggest man in the world. I also have a very sensitive gag reflex.

You see it all the time when you're out in public – a little bastard's throwing a tantrum while mummy is trying to reason with him as if he's got the mental capabilities of an adult. He's screaming away, complaining and crying about Lord knows what while his mother is saying shit like, 'Now, you know that when you eat too much candy your tum-tum gets upset.' Or with an exaggeratedly gentle tone she says, 'If you come with Mummy and stop throwing produce all over the floor of the grocery store we can go get some ice cream when we leave.'

Maybe little Junior doesn't want to leave. Maybe he does. Maybe he wants some candy. Maybe he just wants to fuck with you because you're a useless idiot. Whatever it is, he's not an adult, lady. The only adults that act like that are the adults that need full-time care givers, ride in short buses and wear hockey helmets wherever they go.

But Junior's only three years old so he needs to be dealt with like he's three years old. He doesn't know better than you, or at least I hope to God he doesn't.

If it were up to him, he'd eat candy bars bathed in ice cream, marshmallows and sprinkles for breakfast, lunch and dinner. He'd drink maple syrup instead of milk and he'd never brush his teeth. What I'm trying to say is that he's not that wise yet and he may never be if you keep raising him like he's already a grown man that should just inherently know better. Hell, I'm a grown man and I still rarely know better. My wife needs to kick my ass into line all the time. I'm a real handful, I won't lie.

You spineless douchebags need to stop talking to your children in those irritatingly calm tones while trying to gently reason with them and instead start parenting. Just put a little gusto into it and say 'No' from time to time. And mean it! If you need any help, contact me and I'll put you in touch with my wife. She's a pro. All she ever does is say 'No' to me. It's pretty much her favourite thing to say to me, well that and 'Not tonight.'

I like to think of little kids as if they were dogs. Not because they drool a lot and will eat almost anything off the floor but because it doesn't really matter what it is that you say to them, what matters more is the tone in which you say it.

For instance, let's say that your dog is chewing your shoes. Would you go up to him and in a very calm and deliberate tone say something like, 'Mr. Twinkle Toes, oh Mr. Twinkle Toes, I would really appreciate it if you would be so kind as to stop chewing on my shoes, please. Pretty please. Pretty please with gumdrops and lollipops.'?

Hell no! Well, actually, you douchebag parents I'm talking about probably would, but you're all sack-less losers. So let me tell you what a real man would do. A real man would shout something like 'Brutus, that's enough!' And if that didn't work the first time, well, he'd just yell louder and with more authority the second time, and sure as shit Brutus would stop chewing. The dog doesn't speak English. He merely hears the tone, and the tone means business.

The problem is that these parents to whom I am referring, whose goal is to clearly populate the world with degenerates, do not want to raise their voices to their children. They don't give a shit if their child is screaming in the seat right behind you, kicking the back of your chair without relent on your flight to Mexico. They don't want to raise their voices to tell their kids to shut up and stop, and that's final. Screw the stranger's previously undamaged eardrums, kidneys and chance for a peaceful flight.

It is for this reason that I would like to suggest - as a solution to this epidemic - that we as a society implement a community wide approach to parenting. I propose we use the 'It takes a village to raise a child' philosophy. That would mean if a little rotten child is screaming away behind you on a flight, kicking your seat and really pissing you off, you should be able to speak up. Providing his parents do not after a reasonable amount of time.

I suggest that everyone reading this book start living by this community parenting plan. Give that rotten child's parents a minute to make the child stop. If they don't, then turn around and let the kid, and more importantly the parents, have it. Give them hell!

If we all start doing this together, as a society, in a united front, in time we could make it the norm. I'd love to live in that world. Screaming your lungs out at the little shits and their douchebag parents would sure make most of us feel a whole lot better – kind of like a stress ball. Not only would we relieve the tension caused to us by these little fallen angels, it just may give the little shits that kick in the ass they've been missing their entire lives and put them on the straight and narrow. Either that or it will entice a fist fight with the devil child's parents. But hey, what's life without a little excitement?

Crime and Punishment

OUR JUSTICE SYSTEM, much like many parents of late, has become hopelessly inept. I feel quite confident that at some point in North American history, criminals were actually hesitant to commit crimes. At some point there must have actually been punishments to suit the crimes committed. And I'm willing to bet those punishments probably deterred many potential crimes from taking place.

On the other hand, I'm sure minor indiscretions – such as smoking a joint – were not only legal but were not even frowned upon way back when. However, today we have a system where people have the book thrown at them for hardly a reason at all, and receive next to no sentence for serious and violent crimes. It's as if judges use a magic eight ball to determine sentencing.

In certain countries in the Middle East they will actually cut your hand off if you are convicted of theft. In China, they might actually kill you. If that's not a deterrent to you then nothing is.

Could you imagine if the punishment for rape was castration? If that were the case, I'd be willing to bet that there would be a sudden, sharp and dramatic decline in the number of rapes committed.

All it would take would be for one man to be convicted of rape and have his manhood lopped off to put an end to rape as we know it. There is no question that this punishment would deter every other man in society from ever even considering raping a woman. The new catchphrase would be, 'No means No…or no penis!' And hence, this is the problem with the North American system - the lack of, and sometimes extreme lack of, punishment for serious crimes committed.

Again, I'm not saying that all crimes need harsh punishments. I mean, if you're caught doing something like drinking beer in public in a place where it is illegal to do so, it's not as if anything bad should happen to you because you're not harming a soul with your actions. Honestly, you should be able to drink beer anywhere you like. Some law makers need to chill out, big time. What I'm getting at in this chapter is that serious crimes, crimes where you cause unnecessary pain and suffering to another, need to have severe consequences in order to act as strong deterrents and keep the human garbage off the streets. It's time to take out the trash! (My catchphrase for whenever I run for public office).

Schooling Your Teachers

THE EPIDEMIC lack of respect, authority and punishment has also made its way into schools. I've got a buddy who's a high school teacher and he's told me that some school kids curse openly at many teachers, threaten some teachers and basically do whatever the hell they want. They are above the law.

Schools have tied teachers' hands so much that they can't do anything in retaliation to these students that need to be taught a lesson. If teachers dare discipline these children themselves, the children's douchebag parents might complain. If so, that teacher could potentially lose his or her job.

Don't get me wrong here, not all teachers deserve respect. I had my share of asshole teachers growing up, teachers that would go out of their way to make class an awful experience for everyone.

Some of these teachers were such douchebags that they weren't happy unless all of their students were suffering underneath them. Those teachers deserved all the bad things that would happen to them. You only deserve respect if you are worthy of respect.

I, myself, was no angel, either. I would often go out of my way to make those asshole teachers' lives miserable for attempting to do the same to me. If they wronged me, I would wrong them back tenfold. I'm that petty.

The difference with my childhood behaviour, compared to that of many students today, is that the bad behaviour I exuded periodically was warranted, at least in my mind. I also would never threaten the teachers or curse at them. And there's certainly no way in hell I would have ever physically attacked a teacher. If I had, I would have been suspended from school and my parents would have dealt with me further. That means either my dad would have whooped my ass or I would have been sleeping under a bridge somewhere or both.

And if my behaviour were to have continued, next would have come an expulsion from school. I had seen it happen before so I knew it was a legitimate threat. There were plenty of school suspensions and a couple of expulsions in my school days, so I knew that I could only press those teachers' buttons so much before the shit would hit the fan, even if they were douchebags.

Go back even further in time in the way-back machine to when my parents were in school, and had you told a teacher then to go fuck himself, he would have called you up in front of the class and beaten you with a stick or a belt in plain sight. Now, I'm not saying that was the correct approach, but I'm sure it commanded respect. The problem there, however, was that teachers became power drunk and abused their abusive authority. So there is a fine balance that needs to be in effect. Back then, at least in North America, the teachers had too much power. Now the pendulum has swung too far in the other direction.

You see, the problem with allowing children to act like they are above the law while in school is that, like I wrote earlier, you are setting them up for failure once they get out of school and into the real world.

Wait until little Johnny gets his first job at McDonald's and see what happens to him when his boss asks him to mop soda off the floor of the bathroom and he, instead, tells his boss to go fornicate himself in the restroom. Fired! That's right, precious little Johnny just got his ass fired.

His boss didn't ask him politely to please not speak to him like that. His boss didn't merely take the abuse with a stupid smirk on his face and walk away with his tail between his legs. No, instead Johnny was fired on the spot.

That's real life. Unfortunately for little Johnny, he has never been groomed for real life. As a result, the little shit becomes confused, wondering what the hell just happened because he's never had anything like that happen to him before.

He's been able to act like an out of control asshole in school and with his pathetic parents his entire life and he's never once been so much as scolded for it. But now poor Johnny is perplexed and upset by the situation, not to mention out of a job, thanks in large part to terrible parenting and a ridiculous school system - and the fact that he's a massive jackass.

Our society, as a whole, needs to stop allowing every idiot to walk all over us and start laying down the law. We need to quit bending to everyone's will – to anyone who has an issue with how things are run. Sometimes rules are rules. If you've got a problem with it, tough shit, that's life. Often rules need to be broken too though, but don't get me off topic.

So, what can we do? How can we put the wheels of change in motion? How can we right some of these wrongs I've written about? Well, to begin with I think that douchebag fathers who already have one demon child should not be given the benefit of the doubt. They should, instead, be kicked repeatedly in the scrotum to ensure that they can no longer produce any future degenerate offspring. As for the mothers of these children, well, I don't really know what to do. Surgical sterilization sounds fair. Or perhaps birth control should be dumped into their water without their knowledge. What happens if a woman gets kicked in the uterus by a donkey?

And in the courts, perhaps all judges should be replaced by circus monkeys. The courtroom is a circus anyway, so it would only make sense if feces-throwing monkeys handed down sentences instead of mentally-delayed judges. The sentences handed down by the monkeys couldn't be any more haphazard and irrational than the sentences handed down by actual human judges. Plus, we could pay them in bananas. Think of the savings to tax payers.

CHAPTER 4

GYM ETIQUETTE

You can run into douchebags anywhere. They can be stumbled upon at the grocery store or a restaurant, a movie theater or a concert. But more often than not there seems to be an abundance of them at the gym. For all the pluses that the gym has to offer, those establishments are like a gathering places, or breeding grounds, for some of society's most repellant creatures.

Don't get me wrong, there are all kinds of people that go to the gym: there are wonderful people, horrible people and everyone in between. For instance, I used to go to the gym before I had kids and could actually get out of the house without my wife guilt tripping me about it. Now I have some weights in the garage and pump iron with my boys. What I'm getting at is that I used to go to the gym for years and I am clearly an awesome and amazing human being, so not everyone who goes to the gym is a douchebag. But this book isn't called *The World is Full of Wonderful People*: it's called *Don't Be a Douchebag*.

Many gym folk are fake tanned, steroid inflated, breast augmented, uneducated, egomaniacal sacks of donkey shit. Basically, they're not my kind of people. There are an awful lot of insecure people at the gym whose insecurities manifest in very unpleasant ways.

An awful lot of these specimens like to make a habit of monopolizing as much equipment as they possibly can. They may 'use' two or three different stations, barbells or whatever at the same time, even though they may not be back to any particular one for five or ten minutes, or even at all. The only reason you know that someone is even 'using' that bench press is because someone has thrown a towel over the bar, or left a gym bag on the bench, even though the owner of these items has not been by to claim them for ages.

Sometimes that's not even the case. There are times when there is not even any haphazardly placed gym gear marking the territory. Often enough one of these idiot hoarders is just waiting for you to walk close to their supposed private property. When they see that you are going to use 'their' machine, they shout to you from across the gym or come running up to you to inform you that they are, indeed, using it and that you need to move your ass on. Then to add insult to injury, even though they have gone through all this trouble to move you along, and you have obliged, they won't even hop on it and start using the equipment when you leave. Instead they walk away leaving it once again unattended.

I nearly got into an altercation with a guy at the gym over this very thing one time in the past. Basically, I was already working out but had been eyeing up the squat rack because it was what I wanted to use next. The story goes like this: When I first walked into the gym that day, I noticed that the barbell on the squat rack was on the lowest support and had been loaded with a ton of weight. It was also unattended. I did not, however, want to immediately use it so I went elsewhere for my first workout. I did keep an eye on it though, to see if anyone was indeed using it and had just momentarily left to go get some water.

After ten minutes or so of intensely staring at myself in the mirror as I ferociously grunted out some arm curls, I was done with my first exercise and now wanted to use the squat rack. No one had come to claim it since I had arrived. No one had even gone near it. That meant it was mine for the taking.

So I walked up to the squat rack and, being the conscientious person that I am, looked around yet again in an obvious fashion to see if anyone was approaching. Since there was an awful lot of weight on the bar, I found the only guy within ten yards who I thought was big enough to lift such a load. I asked him if he was using it. He told me that he was not and that he hadn't seen anyone else using it either.

And just like that, it was mine. I took over the station and began to unload the weight from the bar as I wanted to move it up higher on the rack. I had already taken all four plates off of one side of the bar and was halfway through unloading the other side, when this guy walked over to me and told me that he was still using the bar – the bar that I had nearly now unloaded. Quite rudely and abruptly, he instructed me to stop what I was doing and walk away.

Now, I had noticed this guy when I had first walked into the gym and not because he had a hot girl with him or anything like that. I had noticed him because he was wearing the strangest shoes I had ever seen.

They were these rubber shoes that were like gloves, but for your feet. That is probably the best way to describe them - thick rubber gloves for your feet. Each toe was isolated, the rubber wrapping around each toe individually as if they were fingers. I don't care who you are, that's pretty weird and I don't see how it could be at all comfortable. So needless to say, I had already noticed this guy and the first impression hadn't been a good one.

It wasn't merely the fact that he clearly had no right to claim the weight station but also the way in which he spoke to me right from the get go that abrasively rubbed me the wrong way. This dip shit wasn't polite about it. He was completely absent of personality and he had this ridiculous and serious scowl on his face while he spoke to me like a Neanderthal.

He hadn't approached me politely by saying something like, 'Oh, sorry man, I've just got one more set to finish. Do you mind?' Nope, nothing friendly or polite such as that was uttered. He merely marched right up to me with an expressionless look on his douchebag face and said with no inflection in his voice, 'I'm still using that!'

Not being one to oblige such rude behaviour, I looked him up and down with an unimpressed look on my face. He was not that much bigger than me, and definitely not big enough to be lifting all the weight that was on the bar. After a few moments of silence and dirty looks, I spoke.

'No one's been using this for at least ten minutes,' I said, giving him the same emotionless look as I was receiving. 'What were you doing with this bar anyway?' I continued, 'It's got far more weight on it than you could possibly lift, tough guy. Your muscles aren't nearly as hard as that face of yours.'

'I was doing deadlifts,' he said, maintaining his monotone, douchebag voice.

'I guarantee that you couldn't dead-lift what was on the bar if your life depended on it,' I said. 'Anyway, you can't just leave weights on a bar for as long as you like and come back periodically claiming that it's yours and that no one else can use it. This isn't your basement weight set and I'm quite certain you don't own this gym. You don't even own that look on your face. Mr. T. invented that in Rocky III.'

Usually at this point in the conversation a normal human being would apologize to me, probably agree that I was in the right and just back away. Not this douchebag. He was playing for keeps. He, instead, became more aggressive. The moron walked over to a stack of weight plates, took one in hand and then walked back over to me and slide the plate onto the bar that I had just unloaded. Touché!

I'm not going to lie to you, by this point I was getting irritated. My blood pressure had definitely spiked a notch or two and I was about ready to choke the life from the fool. What the prick needed was a good old fashioned ass-whooping and I desperately wanted to be the guy to give him one. I thought about dropping a weight on his stupid foot-glove then popping him with an uppercut. But the mature side of me (which rears its ugly head from time to time) reasoned that even though this guy was a useless douchebag, no good could come from kicking his ass.

Sure, it would have pleased me at that moment, but I would probably have lost my gym membership and potentially had worse consequences to follow had I shit-kicked him. I know, pretty lame, right? I'm not only a disappointment to you the reader, but also to myself. If only I just took artistic liberty to embellish the story, no one would be the wiser. But I'm just too honest a guy. The thing is stories are always better when they are about events where you never considered the consequences before acting. The only thing is that usually in order for that to happen, copious amounts of booze need to be guzzled, and that is usually a bad idea before going to the gym.

So instead of going mental I kept my composure, walked toward him while staring him down, and kept on walking right past him, knocking my shoulder hard into his as I passed, forcing him to take a step back. Even though I wasn't going to kick his ass, that didn't mean I couldn't at least be a little bit of a shit as I left the scene. I do love few things more than pushing people's buttons.

Don't Work Too Hard

THERE ARE PLENTY of self-centered douchebags at the gym that never remove their weights from the bar and put them away when they're done working out. I guess these morons are worried that they may actually break a sweat at the gym if they have to carry those heavy weights all the way back to where they found them.

Here's the thing I really don't get: when you're at the gym you're there to work out, are you not? So wouldn't removing the weights from the bar you were just using, or picking them up off the floor and putting them back in their place only help sculpt your guns that little bit more? Forget about the fact that it's the courteous and right thing to do. I mean, you're in the gym to get in shape and get stronger aren't you? So why put weights on the bar, then lift the bar repeatedly, but not lift them off the bar to put them back where they came from?

The thing is, these douchebags couldn't give a shit about anyone other than themselves. They expect others to deal with the perpetual messes that they leave behind. They don't care if the next person who wants to use that bar may be a tiny woman who may not even be strong enough to unload the large weights left on the bar. But that's not the douchebag's problem, is it?

These are the same people that leave shopping carts in the middle of the parking lot at the grocery store. They are the same people that throw trash onto the ground, even when there is a garbage can nearby. These are the people that let their dogs shit right in the middle of the sidewalk and walk away, pretending like they never even noticed. These losers live with their mothers and their mothers endlessly pick up after them. They're lazy slobs and they bring that behaviour to the gym. Too bad they didn't bring their mothers to the gym as well. But I guess it would be hard to impress the ladies with your mother asking you if you all the time if you need a clean towel and a rub down for your tired muscles, booboo.

Dressed To Impress

THOSE SPECIAL FOLKS at the gym who dress like they're heading immediately to a dance club post workout are, you guessed it, douchebags. When I'm at the gym, I'm wearing an old pair of shorts and a t-shirt that either cost me next to nothing or is so old I would never wear it for any occasion other than to sweat profusely into it.

Some of my workout shirts and shorts are so old and beaten that there's no way a thrift store would take them. They're so abused that if I tried to pass them off to a bum on the street he'd likely take pity on me and insist that I needed the clothes more than he.

All you scum-bag losers who come to the gym to 'workout' with your two hundred dollar jeans, hundred dollar t-shirts and those ugly-ass giant chains around your necks are ridiculous morons. You phony douchebags need to be stopped. I find you all to be more irritating that jock itch and more obnoxious than Bill Belichick. If only there was a powder they could sprinkle around the perimeter of the gym that would keep you all away.

Many of these idiots to which I am referring spend their entire time at the gym on their cell phones. That right there is a big red flag. That is an insurmountable character flaw. Your phone should be stowed in the locker room, the same place that your ridiculous jeans should have been. I mean honestly, who works out in jeans? For all that science has done for the world I guess there's still no cure for stupid.

Now, the only thing worse than sharing floor space with one of these imbeciles is to be inflicted - nay, assaulted - by one of their inane phone conversations. These douchebags only speak at full volume, giving you no choice but to overhear everything. A dullard like this will boast about how he picked up some 'bitch' at the club the night prior, which all fellow gym members know to be an utter and complete lie due to the fact that this misfit couldn't even seal the deal with a lady he procured from a seedy street corner.

I don't know why the gym entices so many horrible human beings, but I guess that's just the way the cookie crumbles. Douchebags will forever be drawn to the gym, like moths to the flame. Oh, if only those douchebags could also be drawn to the flame.

CHAPTER 5

DRIVING ME CRAZY

When I was but knee high to a grasshopper, all I wanted to do was drive. I was obsessed. Anything that had a big, loud engine in it could do no wrong by me. I was like an addict and my drug of choice went vroom!

I was so enamoured with driving that I took each and every opportunity presented to me to get behind the wheel of anything I could, whether I was invited to or not. Often enough, my dad would let me stand on his lap and steer his truck at our home, or at least pretend to steer it. I probably thought I was doing a whole hell of a lot more than I actually was. Regardless, I was hooked. I was so crazy that I even crashed my first vehicle when I was but three years old. Now how many people can boast about that? I didn't even wait until I had pubes or a girl to impress before I got into a smash up.

The story goes like this: I had been left alone, for a mere moment or two, in my father's running pickup truck in the driveway of our home. It was a 70's model Chevrolet pickup with a bench seat. If I remember correctly, it was blue. Being the clever child that I was, the moment I was alone I took the opportunity to hop over to the driver's seat. Might as well take the old truck for a spin, I must have reasoned. What a good boy I was.

While standing on the driver's seat, I started playing with the shifter on the steering column. I managed to pop it into neutral, I suppose, and the truck began to roll down the slope of our driveway. We lived on a decent sized piece of property in the country, so it was quite a long driveway. Standing on that seat with the steering wheel in my hands and rolling down the hill, in that moment I was probably the happiest child on the planet. I was also on a crash course, heading directly towards a work truck that was parked at the bottom of the hill.

When my dad – who had popped into the garage to get something – heard the truck's tires roll, he turned around and was startled to see me bouncing up and down, joyfully, on the driver's seat as I steered the thing away. Shocked by what was unfolding in front of him, he ran off after me at a full sprint.

When he caught up to the truck, he swung the driver's door open, pushed me aside and hopped in to apply the brake. He was, however, a second too late as we connected with the parked truck.

Upon impact, I was thrown to the floor of the passenger seat. I was told that I had a wild look on my face, obviously waiting to see if I was going to get in trouble. Or perhaps I was just so exhilarated from what I had accomplished. I think I sprouted my first chest hair that day. As soon as my dad told me that he wasn't mad at me and he just wanted to know if I was okay, I was apparently happy as a pig in shit about my achievement - my first solo drive. I was quite proud of myself. I still am.

But that was then and this is now. I no longer have that youthful exuberance each and every time I get an opportunity to drive. Now that I'm a grown man and I drive in the city, things have changed a little. Actually, things have changed a lot. I no longer love driving if I have to drive downtown. I feel like a paranoid schizophrenic when I drive in the city, as if everyone is out to get me.

I feel that way even more so when riding my motorbike. My head's always on a swivel when I'm on my hog. I don't even think I'm exaggerating when I say that roughly one hundred percent of other drivers go out of their way to try their best to nail me when I'm on my bike. I spend half my ride time on the road avoiding the plethora of morons that clog the roadways and attempt to change lanes into me. I'm sure many of you can relate to this. Those of you who can't relate are probably the crazy, reckless assholes that the rest of us struggle daily to avoid. May you continue to live in blissful ignorance.

It's funny to me to observe how people's true colours come to light once they get behind the steering wheel of a vehicle. For some reason, as soon as certain people hop in the car and turn the key, an abrupt change in personality takes place. Like booze to an angry drunk, driving simply brings out the worst in certain people.

Like most people have probably experienced, I've been driving along, minding my own business only to suddenly have some asshole recklessly cut right in front of me in traffic and then proceed to flash me his middle finger with an irate ferocity. Hell, it's not even always a dude. I've seen women do this too. I think those chicks have been drinking too much steroid water or something. They must shave their tits and chew tobacco because normal chicks don't behave that way.

Needless to say, these idiots were apparently pissed off by my mere presence on the road and they made their disdain for me perfectly clear with an angry face and a crude hand gesture. Some were even yelling in their vehicles, fuming with rage. That's not healthy behaviour. Granted, incidents like these have only happened to me a handful of times over the years, but even one such unprovoked incident will taint you.

Perhaps these dip shits would have noticed me had they bothered to signal and shoulder check before changing lanes, but who am I to judge? I personally like to take a look over my shoulder before moving lanes in traffic, but there I go making sense again. Instead, these morons tried to remove the front bumper from my vehicle and flip me off in the process, all for nothing, for no gain at all. A little toot of my horn to warn them that they were about to collide with me was enough to send them off the deep end.

This behavioural display, particularly when perpetrated by someone much smaller or weaker or less manly than myself, strikes me as being especially hilarious. I highly doubt that the scrawny little pencil-necked geek who flagrantly cut me off, screamed, cursed me out and flashed his middle finger my way with pure hatred in his eyes and a horror movie scowl on his face would partake in the same behaviour if, instead of driving, we were both walking down the sidewalk together.

Just picture it: a complete stranger and I are both walking down the street, him on the left and me on the right side of the sidewalk. I'm a little behind him but I am walking faster than he is. I am gradually catching up to him and will overtake him shortly.

As I approach and am about to overtake him, he decides that he is no longer satisfied walking down the left side of the curb we share and is now more fond of the right side. So he moves over abruptly to his right, almost striking me with his man-purse in the process.

He doesn't bother to look before moving over. He doesn't bother to turn his head to see where he is going and to ensure that no obstacles are in his way. He merely moves over quickly while looking in the opposing direction.

Then suddenly, he notices me directly on his ass and he stops abruptly for no reason at all. I get up on my toes and stop quickly so that I don't flatten him. Then in a sudden fit of rage, he turns around and sticks his middle finger right into my face and tells me to go fuck myself. He then turns around and starts walking again, this time swaggering from left to right, blocking me so that I am now unable to walk past him on either side.

Nothing like that would ever happen. I couldn't really picture anyone doing such a thing other than, perhaps, a cracked-out drug addict whose paranoid delusions have convinced him that magic fairies are after him and he has to scare them off in order to score another fix.

So here's the thing: if you wouldn't do it on the street without a steel cage around you, why then as soon as you get behind the wheel of a car do you take on the persona of a roid-raging maniac. Kind of like a Chihuahua's misguided portrayal of its own size and strength, this douche now thinks that he is ten feet tall and bullet proof sitting in his car.

A fool like that needs a serious reality check, and one day he may pop his middle finger up at the wrong guy and get his due. Either that or his incredible rage is going to cause a massive brain aneurism to blow. I'm praying for the latter. Karma is a wonderful thing.

Bicycle Daredevils

WHILE I'M ON the subject of douchebag behaviour in traffic, I feel it only fair to mention the bicycle rider. Before I go any further, I should mention that I often cycle to work. I also have a couple buddies who cycle to work, from time to time. As a result, I can't paint all cyclists with the same brush. However, there are a good number of bicycle douchebags out there that are absolute menaces.

These cyclists have absolutely no regard for any other person. Hell, many of them don't even appear to have any regard for their own lives or personal safety. I'm pretty sure some must be suicidal, because they sure ride like it.

When I ride to work, I wear a cycling coat that's bright and reflective. I also have a flashing headlight and taillight on my bike. That's because I enjoy living. I don't want to be creamed by a car. I don't want to be a human pancake. I don't look like the most badass dude on the planet when I ride, but what I do look like is a man who will ride another day.

These bicycle daredevils have a slightly different approach. To begin with, some like to blend into the background. If it's dark and grey out, dark and grey coloured clothing will be what they're wearing. I like to ride the same way I drive. They, on the other hand, dart in and out of traffic and blindly cut in front of moving vehicles at will, as if there is an invisible protective bubble around them that will somehow keep them safe if and when they make contact with two thousand pounds of rolling steel.

These morons cycle on roads, sidewalks and crosswalks. They blow through red lights, stop signs and basically exhibit whatever nut job behaviour they please, like an unsupervised two year old hopped up birthday cake and ice cream. They ride with traffic, against traffic, and act as if they have the rights of vehicles, pedestrians and cop cars all rolled into one. Except they aren't walking, they aren't driving, and they sure as shit aren't out there protecting and serving like the men and ladies in blue.

I have had numerous close calls with bicycle riders over the years while driving, and I am always impressed with the incredible disregard that many of them have towards self-preservation. Even when I was a child out riding my bike, I had more between my two ears than these adult aged bicycle douchebags.

I also liked to do my fair share of stupid things on my bike when I was young, as I'm sure most boys do. I used to make dirt jumps. When the jumps became too easy to handle I would increase the difficulty level by trying to land the jumps while standing on my seat or in some other stupid and awkward position. Sometimes I would launch into a jump with no hands on the handle bars and just hope that things would work out. Things didn't always work out, but I survived and amazingly with no broken bones to tally.

I would also try to surf my bike down the street when I was six or seven years old, one foot on the handle bars and another on the seat. This also periodically ended in a crash, but that never discouraged me from trying again. Maybe I had a screw loose. My wife seems to think I have a few.

One thing that I did seem to understand, even though I was sometimes a little daredevil, was that falling off my bike and hitting the ground was one thing, but being hit by a moving car was a whole other problem. If I played chicken with a car or if I cut one off on the street and gave it no other option but to hit me, I knew I would lose that confrontation.

Even a little child can understand that eighty pounds of boy and bike does not stand a skittle's chance in fat camp against a few thousand pounds of car and driver. So I made my jumps and I did my stupid little stunts, but I always knew that road rash and bruises were more or less the biggest risks I ever ran.

Why is it then that these full grown douchebags, even the ones with all their silly-looking fluorescent spandex and aerodynamic helmets, can't understand what I had figured out when I was only six years old? It's because they are self-absorbed douchebags with demented senses of entitlement. They know they're dangerously cutting in front of you in traffic, all while moving slower than you are in your car, but they trust that you will see them and will stop in time. They are morons. They are evolutionary throwbacks.

I think that putting your own life in the hands of a stranger behind the wheel of a car, a stranger who may or may not be paying attention to you or even realize that you exist, is about as intelligent as lighting a cigarette while filling up your vehicle at the gas pump. One of these days, that driver you flagrantly cut off might have his attention on something other than your spandex-clad ass and run you over. Maybe he'll have his attention on a sexy lady's yoga pant ass as she's jogging by and he'll unknowingly flatten you with a smile on his face.

Or maybe you'll meet another douchebag, one who happens to be texting while driving. It would be a meeting of the morons. That confrontation could actually be a positive one for the world, though. That smash up would result in one less douchebag taking up space and perhaps land a dangerous driver in jail. Lucky for you though, that goofy-coloured spandex you've covered your body with will surely save your life if and when a collision does occur. I mean, why else would you be wearing it? It couldn't be just to make a statement, unless the statement you're trying to make is that you have no taste or sense of embarrassment. Because those head to toe flamboyant, colour splattered spandex get ups are about as awful to look at as a live birth video in a labour and delivery class.

Helmet Schmelmet

THE HELMET is a paradoxical piece of equipment. It can make situations better, but at the same time make them much worse. The purpose of a helmet is to protect us from cracking our skulls open while participating in skull cracking activities. So, instead of avoiding these dangerous activities or exercising a little bit of caution while performing them, we strap on a helmet, go full tilt and hope for the best.

Helmets give many people a false sense of invincibility. It's as if they believe that the smashing of their head into a tree, onto the ice or the ground while wearing a helmet will result in no pain or suffering whatsoever. That's why I say that helmets can hurt as much as they can help.

Before helmets were around, people would limit themselves in the stupid behaviour department. When I was a small boy, nobody wore a bicycle helmet. I know I sound like your grandpa right now, walking barefoot, uphill both to and from school in three feet of snow, but it's true. That was in the 80's. Bicycle helmets have really only been around and popular for twenty to twenty five years or so. Or at least the first time that I ever saw a bicycle helmet was about twenty some odd years ago when I was in third or fourth grade. It was the early 90's.

People have always pulled stupid stunts while bicycle riding, skateboarding, or playing ice hockey, to name a few skull crunching activities. But I think the invention of helmets in sports merely amped up the level of stupidity and aggressiveness displayed…and injuries.

Before the helmet, people felt somewhat vulnerable. For instance, kids like me used to show a certain level of restraint when performing dumb stunts.

We knew that if we smashed our skulls to the ground we'd be messed up, so we tried our best to not. But with the onslaught of the helmet, the worry of smashing the head seemed to disappear, or at least be placed on the back burner.

The risks taken while performing stunts became greater and greater as protective gear improved, resulting in creative and more spectacular accidents and injuries. No one used to do back flips on their bikes. Now people back flip snow mobiles because they feel almost invincible with all the protective gear they wear. But they're not. Necks still get broken. Brains still get damaged – the extreme popularity of low-class reality television is all I need to reference as a shining example of that.

That brings me to one of the dumbest laws that have ever been implemented, the helmet law. Why do we need a helmet law? Why should we force people who vehemently do not want to comply to wear helmets while riding motorbikes and bicycles? Like Jerry Seinfeld so cleverly stated, 'The point of (the helmet law) is to protect a brain that is functioning so poorly, it's not even trying to stop the cracking of the head that it's in.'

Darwin's theory referred to this as natural selection. We, as a society, are interfering with nature, or natural selection, by creating and enforcing these silly sorts of laws. I don't feel it should be the job of society to have to protect morons from themselves. A law such as this helps to prolong the lives of idiots and permit them to survive longer than nature possibly intended, allowing them a greater potential to procreate. It gives the foolish douchebags of the world an increased opportunity to create even more stupid offspring to populate the planet.

I suggest we get rid of laws like the helmet law. Creating and enforcing laws of this nature will only help society to regress, not progress. Intelligent people will most likely choose to protect their noggins when riding their motorcycles, regardless of a law, while morons may not.

If you want to protect yourself with a helmet while riding a bicycle, but more importantly while riding a motorcycle, that's great, I recommend it. But if you don't want to, I don't care and neither should the law.

If you are dumb enough to want to ride your motorcycle while wearing shorts, a t-shirt, running shoes and no helmet, then please be my guest. You won't catch me riding like that, but hey, that's just me. I guess I kind of value my own health and existence a little more than some others do. I just don't understand why we go to the extent that we do to protect people from themselves. Of all the things we could use more of in this world, morons and douchebags are not among them.

In the jungle, if a lion attacks a pack of gazelles and the gazelles all run away with the exception of one who just stays put, that lone gazelle will most likely be dinner. Maybe the pack is better off without that one. It's clearly not too bright and its existence merely makes the pack weaker instead of stronger.

Therefore, if someone thinks it's a good idea to ride their motorbike down the highway doing a hundred miles an hour without any protection, so be it. If the brain's not even intelligent enough to exude self-preservation in the face of potential hazard, then why does society feel a need to step up and protect it? I think we should let nature take its course. Call me cold-hearted if you will, but I prefer to be called old-fashioned. I'm just tired of the ever increasing percentage of idiots that I seem to have to deal with on a day to day basis. Don't fuck with nature, helmet law.

CHAPTER 6

WALK THIS WAY

MAYBE I'M CRAZY, but I've always adhered to the old mantra of look both ways before you cross the street. I probably had a firm grasp of that concept by the time I entered kindergarten. So why is it that on a regular basis I see people from all different walks of life step off the curb, directly into traffic, without even looking?

Sometimes it's on a cross walk, sometimes it's in the middle of the street. Either way, it's mental not to check to see if something's going to smash you to death before you step off a curb onto a street.

While a person crossing the street at an actual crosswalk may, indeed, have the technical right of way, is it better to prove a point and die or to have a look and live? The answer may appear obvious to me, but perhaps I have a skewed vantage point. I mean, I want to live to breathe another day. I want to taste another beer, eat another pound of bacon, see another naked lady - and by 'naked lady' I mean my wife, of course (there's a very slim chance she may one day read this and I don't want that day to be my last). I want to do all of those things and many more, several more times in my life. As a result, I always take a peak to see what's coming before stepping into the path of death-mobiles. As crazy as it seems to me, I regularly see people who have a different take on it.

These idiots get hit with a stunning regularity. Often enough, on the news, I will hear of yet another pedestrian being struck and killed by a car. And while the news sometimes takes a skewed vantage point, the person my heart goes out to, unless it truly wasn't the fault of the pedestrian, is the driver. Such an event can be a traumatic experience for the driver who flattened a dude.

But these douchebag jaywalkers lack the intelligence to think far enough ahead as to the potential consequences of their actions. They are not even smart enough to realize that they could actually get hit by a car and die by stepping into moving traffic. They are clearly so mentally distorted that they assume that every car on the road is paying full and complete attention to them and will, therefore, stop or evade them.

Not only do these knuckleheads cross the street without looking, but just to piss you off that extra inch, the cream of the bonehead crop will cross at a snail's pace. You see it all the time while driving in the city: someone's walking at a normal pace, but as soon as their foot leaves the sidewalk and they have the opportunity to obstruct traffic, they slow to half their previous speed until they have reached the other side of the street.

When I see people crossing the street in this fashion, I see it as if they've just challenged me to a game of chicken. Challenge accepted! I don't like to lose.

Now, I don't want to kill anybody, but I do like teaching douchebags a lesson when I get the opportunity. So when I see someone crossing the street in front of me – a real douchebag who's not on a cross walk nor is even looking at me or hurrying up about it, a douchebag that just wants to make me come to a stop in the middle of the street to prove his power - I do not slow down or change my course of direction. Instead, I continue to drive at the same speed and in the same path that I was before I noticed the knuckle dragger sauntering across the road.

Barrelling down upon the douchebag jaywalker, I wait until the last possible second to make the most minimal turn of the steering wheel to avoid hitting the dimwit. Instead of swerving wide, I try to come within a couple feet of making contact with him. Then, as I pass him by - so closely that he feels the force of vehicular wind push at him - I lay on my horn.

Usually when I perform this manoeuvre, I can actually see the douchebag's life flash before his eyes and his pants fill with excrement, all in one fell swoop. I've got to say, it really makes me feel better about the entire situation. It just fills me with joy.

I get so pissed off at these self-absorbed losers. They think they can command traffic just because they fucking feel like it. Not on my watch! Attempting to give each and every one of them a heart attack is how I vent and keep my sanity. It's my therapy session. I get a real kick out of it if I can make just one of these idiots shit themselves in the middle of the street. I mean, that's exactly what they're trying to do to drivers. I'm merely turning the tables on them. I am an amazing man!

You're Not Alone In This World

HAVE YOU EVER BEEN walking down the sidewalk towards a group of three or so people who are all meandering abreast to each other, and as you approach they refuse to do so much as to acknowledge your presence? They are blocking one hundred percent of the sidewalk, extending from one edge to the other in a human chain, yet as you close in on the group, not a one of them attempts to make way for you to pass. Instead, they all keep sauntering in your direction, blocking your path while looking anywhere but directly at you. They clearly have no other goal in mind than to force you from the sidewalk. Either that or you've got a bigger problem as you appear to have actually become invisible.

I don't know when it became the norm to expect the worst from people, but sadly, that's what I expect. I now find myself feeling surprised whenever I encounter someone who is genuinely nice and considerate. If someone actually moves out of my way to allow me to pass by, it surprises me a little. That's how bad it's gotten. I blame the immigrants!

Sometimes, I get so tired of dodging douchebags (or douchebag dodging, as they say in France) that I start playing a little game, much like my traffic game, except this time I'm not driving a wrecking ball on wheels so I don't move. It doesn't matter who's coming at me, once I've reached the point of being utterly fed up with dodging the plethora of assholes that keep walking into me, I decide to stop moving for any of them.

It could be a mammoth man or a pubescent hormone, when they are walking straight at me and I know they're just pretending not to notice me, I also pretend to not notice them. Most of the time the guilty party will move at the last second so they don't quite bump into me, but sometimes they really stick hard to their game, assuming that I will stop or move aside. But I don't. At this point I have fully committed, so I just look off into the distance and tense up, bracing for impact. These douchebags aren't expecting me to be so rock solid upon impact, so when they connect with me, they feel it.

I have knocked the shit out of people doing this - figuratively speaking, for the most part - and it has really melted away my stress (crowded areas can tend to stress me out). These douchebags deserve a little thumping so I don't feel bad about it at all. I have knocked people flat on their asses or have spun them like tops because they've walked straight into me, on purpose, when I had nowhere else to go.

Try it sometime. Just maybe not on little tiny grandmas though. Even if they are begging for it, their bones are made of dust and they will, literally, explode if you smash them. Self-centered meat heads who like to play chicken, on the other hand, are more densely put together and they are certainly not expecting you to be solid as your grandfather's brick shit house when they strike you. So it really catches them off guard when they bounce off of you. It can also get you some great reactions. Consider it a lesson learned for the douchebag, a lesson that's a really satisfying one to teach. Go unto the world, my pupils, and spread the knowledge!

CHAPTER 7

THE DIGITAL AGE

CALL ME old fashioned, but I'm not always the biggest fan of technology. All these devices that are invented to simplify our lives seem to achieve the exact opposite at times. And I find it irritating how computers and cell phones are ever-changing, often in the minutest of ways.

How can I buy something that is state of the art one year, only to have it be nothing but worthy of the garbage bin the next? Sometimes it doesn't even take so much as a year to become obsolete. It can be a matter of months or weeks until it becomes outdated. That's bullshit.

It's a scam, a scam perpetrated by technology companies, I tells ya! They make little tweaks or come up with new gimmicks every few months or so to keep the consumer hooked and coming back for more. The is no limit to the amount of unnecessary shit people will buy.

Why should I spend all my time learning how to use the latest and greatest technology only for it all to change in a matter of months? How much free time do these companies think I have? More than that, how much money do they think we all have oozing from our pockets?

Technology companies like to jerk the masses around. They are constantly brainwashing us with advertisements that convince us we need to keep buying bigger, better-looking, newer and faster products. Is there really anything wrong with the phone you bought last year? According to the Teddy, the tech nerd you work with, there sure fucking is! But do you actually need to shell out a ton more cash to replace your phone simply because the newest model has a camera that is, almost imperceptibly, better and has a screen that is one centimeter larger? Maybe I sound a little old school here, but I don't really need to burn my paycheck in order to replace my current phone with the new state-of-the-art one that comes in three fun new colours!

And it is absolutely amazing to me how text-messaging has completely taken over the word. Now I've got to be honest, a few years back I didn't understand why texting was so popular. That was when I had an old school flip phone. Then one day I got a new phone that made texting easy - a smart phone, as they call it - and I saw the appeal. I was converted…well, to a point. I don't know about the rest of you, but I can't type as quickly as I can speak. This is especially true when I am using only my thumb to type on a tiny little keypad. Granted, text messaging does have its place, and I do use it a lot, but it shouldn't completely consume your life. If it has, may God save your soul.

Part of the problem with texting is the amount of useless shit that people text to each other and the copious amount of time wasted. Never at any other time in history would somebody have dialed up their friend on the phone just to say, 'Eating ice cream. Yum!' and abruptly ended the call. Then, two minutes later, phoned back again to say, 'Hair elastics rule!' only to hang up again. But for some reason people now feel the need to constantly text the most pointless statements to each other. As if I give a shit what you had for dessert! I'm a grown man. Text me a joke or a set of tits and call it quits.

Regardless of how ridiculous I think it is, many people have become dangerously obsessed with text messaging. Some are willing to risk life and limb just to text a pointless comment to a friend. There have been countless fatal car accidents because people have had their eyes on their phones instead of the road.

Take a look around the next time you're parked at a red light. If you're looking for it, you'll eventually spot many people sitting there looking down at their laps. All these people look like they've been hypnotized by the tiny phone screens, unable to break eye contact as if a spell has been placed on them. But to me, sitting beside them at the red light, it just looks like they're really into their crotches.

These text messaging zombies seldom ever lift their heads, uncaring as to the obstacles that may lie ahead. Nothing is more important than their phones to them, not even arriving alive to their destination.

And it's far from just drivers who text at inappropriate times. I saw a mother in a museum once, ignoring her tyrant children because of her love affair with her hand held device. It didn't matter to her that the little fuckers were on a maniacal rampage in and amongst priceless artifacts. She was apparently oblivious - or merely uncaring - to the destruction her kids were perpetrating, all because of the magic spell her phone had cast upon her.

Over a period of several minutes she didn't even look up to see what the hell her little maniacs were up to. Who cares if little Billy is about to destroy an ancient artifact from Guatemala? Don't worry about raising and teaching your kids, lady. I'm sure they'll be just fine without you. Their phones can probably teach them a whole lot more than their negligent mother.

Text messaging has clearly begun to erode social skills in children as well as adults. I don't even think that school-aged boys know how to talk to girls anymore. I saw two high school kids out on what I assumed was a date, sitting side by side, texting. I can only imagine that instead of speaking to each other they were texting back and forth. What a sad and pathetic display that was to behold. If that's the best the boy can do, I don't know how he's ever going to get laid. Human contact and interaction is apparently going the way of the cassette tape. I feel like an old man. I'm cantankerous and don't even want to look at my phone for at least the next minute. Ok, I give in. Where is that damn thing? Maybe I have an lol from a bff?

Death By Text

A WHILE BACK, I was driving up the I-5 through Seattle. Within a timespan of no more than a minute, two different cars blatantly cut me off. Both were travelling under the speed limit, but I was driving faster when they cut me off. If it weren't for my cat-like reflexes, I would have rear-ended them both. Needless to say, my brakes earned their price tag in that minute.

Neither driver had a clue that I was on the highway. They couldn't have, because they weren't looking out of their vehicles – behaviour typically not recommended while driving. They both had their eyes locked on their cell phones. Neither driver shoulder-checked nor bothered to signal to let me know they were moving over. What's even worse is that neither of them even looked away from their phones before, during, or after changing lanes. To be honest, I don't know if either one of them was even aware that they had changed lanes. They sure as hell didn't notice that they'd nearly lost their lives.

Apparently for these two geniuses, text messaging trumps living. Now, I don't care if they want to kill themselves. It would make absolutely no difference in my life if a stranger offed himself. But the fact that they tried to take me with them on their journey to hell really pissed me off. That got me hoping they would change lanes into each other. With their heads down and noses buried in their phones, both cars could have bumped and rolled violently off the freeway, bursting into flames as they came to rest, just like in the movies. It would have been poetic justice.

If these people can't even place their text messaging addictions on hold driving the highway, they certainly won't be able to refrain while walking down the street. Some people are so hooked, I once saw a dude walk into a telephone pole while texting. He was too stupid to look away from his phone to notice the immovable object directly in his path. The saddest part is that he's probably done it before and will probably do it again. It's a pretty safe bet because after the impact I saw him rub his head wound, shake off the impact, and continue on his way with his face buried in his phone. The pain and embarrassment of colliding with a telephone pole didn't even cause him to put his phone away. That's a special kind of a man right there.

This brings me back to the original purpose of the phone, which was...wait for it, kids...to talk to people. Why doesn't anyone want to do this anymore? I'm pretty sure that you can walk down the street without marching into people or telephone poles if you are talking on your phone. I know that may seem pretty crazy or revolutionary to some of you, but it's a hell of a lot easier. And instead of texting while driving, talk. Bluetooth comes in every care these days. Just use it and stop endangering the lives of all whom you encounter.

And here's a lesson for the socially stunted: if someone is talking to you in person, face to face, give them priority over the person you are texting with. If you don't want to be considered a huge douchebag, make eye contact with the person speaking with you and put your phone away for a moment. Don't let texting control your life. That's what wives are for.

Curbing My Bullshit

WITH EVERYONE having instant internet access at their fingertips, it's becoming harder and harder to exaggerate the truth. It used to be a lot easier to bullshit people. I miss those good old days.

I remember the good old days, long before smartphones were so common place (I'm talking like 5 years ago here, ancient history). I could be out with buddies at the pub, and we'd be shooting the shit and telling each other war stories, often with heavy doses of hyperbole thrown in. The more beer we poured down our gullets, the taller our tales would become. Basically, normal guy shit.

Personal exploits, sports talk or anything else could have been the subject on the table. As tales would increasingly grow in exaggeration, eventually someone would call bullshit. The details would then be argued about over more pints. But it didn't matter because no one could check the facts at the pub. That was the fun of it. There was a mystic to it that was wonderful.

That was back when ignorance was bliss and a tall tale could remain just that. Computers were only at home on your office desk or locked up in a briefcase in your car, not in your jeans' pocket, carried with you at all times.

These days everyone out there has a phone that doubles as a computer, a camera, a video camera, an MP3 player, a videogame console and a day planner. Now, I'm not saying that's not cool, because it's actually pretty amazing. What I'm saying is that certain times and places call for them to be left behind.

Part of the problem with so many people carrying mutated phones is that they enable you to perform immediate fact checking. You may be reading this right now and saying to yourself, 'Hey, isn't that a good thing?' Well let me tell you that it's not always.

A few years ago you could have exaggerated how many knockouts Mike Tyson had in his career or how tall Sylvester Stallone really is, while out with the boys. But today if one of your buddies has a smart phone and actually uses it like a nerdy fact-checking douchebag, he can check your facts right then and there. While you're elbow deep into a plate of hot wings, he can point out that you were indeed wrong about the actual score of last weekend's football game and that you were also wrong about how many farewell tours KISS has performed. Now, what fun is that? No one likes a know-it-all.

Basically, what I'm getting at here is that technology is ruining a bullshitter's ability to bullshit. When your facts can be checked anytime, anywhere, it can really put a damper on your storytelling abilities. Like a wise man once said, never let the truth get in the way of a good story.

The irritating thing about these so-called *smart* phones is that no argument is ever left unsettled. You and a friend could again be at the pub (why would you ever be anywhere else) arguing about how many goals Wayne Gretzky scored in his career. It used to be that after a good hour or so of drunken debate and incessant back and forth put-downs, you would have both consumed enough beer to forgot what was being argued about in the first place. Maybe a hot waitress would walk by, distracting you both from a pointless conversation with her amazing cleavage. Then you would order more beer and try to solve some more of the world's mysteries.

But these days, your buddy may just have one of those cursed smart phones on him and pull it out and use it at the mere mention of a discrepancy - well before a good old-fashioned and pointless drunken argument could even take place.

When going out with the guys, all technology should be left behind. Make it a rule with your buddies that any device with the word 'smart' in its description be left at home. That way, for one thing, no one's lady can keep tabs on them. For another thing, no one can preoccupy all their time by playing with their phone instead of socializing.

If you get into a pointless argument with a buddy and he pulls out his smartphone to try to interject his precious 'facts,' you should remove his phone from his person and drown it in a jug of beer. At least it will die a happy death and you will have finally won a battle with technology.

CHAPTER 8

I GET AROUND

PUBLIC TRANSIT SUCKS. Most students can't afford a car and are, therefore, forced to take the bus. During my college years, in which I spent a great deal of time riding mass transit, I came up with a theory about public transportation. I'm quite certain they make it as shitty as it is in order to be a form of subliminal message to students. 'Work hard, get a good job and you will never have to ride in this pile of trash bus again.'

There is nothing enjoyable about public transit. Quite often it's overcrowded to the point where your only riding option is to cozy up to a group of weirdoes standing near the entrance and be gently molested along the journey. To boot, so many people who use transit are rude and obnoxious douchebags, their pleasant demeanours adding nothing but joy to the already unpalatable experience of being crammed into a tight space with hordes of strangers.

There is usually one token degenerate crammed nice and tight in there next to you who smells like he's sworn of bathing for life. This wretched douchebag single-handedly putrefies the entire train. He smells like he hasn't taken a shower since Jesus last walked the earth, but that doesn't stop him from getting out and living his life. I truly don't know how these people live with themselves. Do they have no sense of smell or are they merely immune to their own vile stench? Are they allergic to showering or do they have a phobia of soap and clean water?

And don't forget about the requisite nut job, crack head, and schizophrenic who frequent public transit. Because what is a ride on the subway without some mental case freaking out, shouting and having a full blown argument with himself and his split personalities?

To add yet another layer of enjoyment to public transportation, the heaters on the buses and trains are often broken in the winter and the air conditioning always craps out in the summer. Depending on where you live, taking trains and buses can almost take longer than walking to your destination. Huge detours and frequent stops and delays are the norm.

Yet there are commercials on TV and the radio to suggest we use public transit instead of driving our cars to help save the environment. But with all these downsides I listed above, why would anyone who can afford a car ever take the bus?

Maybe if they revamped their ad campaigns they might have a shot with their attempts to increase ridership. Advertisements like, 'No shower, no ride!' or 'Forgot your meds, forget the train!', might help, because if things stay the way they are, no one who can avoid it will ever use public transportation willingly.

Crowded out

I REALLY DON'T CARE for crowds. I'm just putting that out there so you know where I'm coming from. I'm a man who likes his personal space. I love freedom, peace and quiet. I enjoy being away from the hustle and bustle.

Now, I don't suffer from agoraphobia or anything like that, I just like my space - at least most of the time. The thing is, there are times when where I want to be or what I want be doing requires being near swarms of people. And not all crowds are created equal.

Sometimes you're in a crowd where everyone is doing their best to get along. Usually that's when you all have a vested interest. A prime example is a crowd leaving a football game, on their way home, celebrating victory.

Other times, you're in a crowd full of douchebags that are bumping into one another, shouting, yelling, picking fights and just outright pissing you off by being gratuitous assholes. Often enough, those same degenerates who ride transit without having showered in years are now smack dab in the middle of a crowd, doing their best to pollute the air.

If you, like me, are not the biggest fan of being in really crowded areas, these douchebags will, without a doubt, seek you out like a hound dog does a coon. If you're out at a hockey game, they will inevitably end up sitting behind you. These idiots will spew their fifty-word vocabulary at the top of their lungs while kicking the back of your chair and occasionally spilling beer and popcorn onto your shoulder.

This behaviour can push you close to the edge. You're already tense from riding in on the train and fighting the crowd into the arena. But don't lose your cool. Even though the vocabulary-challenged chronic beer spiller is a massive douchebag, he may also be a steroid inflated bag of wind. So, before you snap, assess the situation…and the size of the dude. A little beer on your clothing is much better than a lot of your own blood. Use your brain.

Taxi Driver

NO MATTER WHAT country you travel to, there are likely to be taxis waiting at the airport upon your arrival. Lined up like a herd of pigs to the trough, there they await hungry to be fed by your tourist dollars. From my experience, taxi drivers are among the craziest bastards on the road.

Years ago, when I was in Mexico, I learned a life lesson for future dealings with cab drivers, especially cab drivers in Third World countries where rules I am familiar with may not apply. I had just wrapped-up a pub crawl with a few guests from the resort I had been staying at. The bars had all closed and I was eager to get back to my hotel for some more food and drink.

I got into a cab and told the Mexican cabbie something that I began to regret within a minute of saying it. I told the man to take me back to my hotel - and to step on it. I also mentioned to him that I wanted to get back before the people in the other cab did. That was a huge mistake. Hindsight is a motherfucker.

With a nod and a smile, he tore off like a demented NASCAR driver accelerating out of the pit. It was as if he was Bandit and had just been radioed with the news that another Smokey was hot on his tail. No shoulder check, no seat belt, just pedal to the floor and off we went. As fast as that little piece-of-shit car could move, it did.

As my head was thrown back with as much force as a 4 cylinder beater can deliver. There were cars in front of us. They were driving rather slowly in our lane up the cobblestone street. I use the word 'lane' loosely here, because I don't really think that lanes exist in Mexico. In my brief experience, people there seem to drive wherever the hell they want to, in whatever direction they want to, much of the time.

Anyway, there were cars in our lane impeding our progress, but there were no cars coming towards us in the oncoming lane. So, my taxi driver, Speedy Gonzales, decided to drive up the wrong side of the small city street in order to pass the procession of cars. Caution to the wind, he held that gas pedal down firmly as we flew past the other cars on the narrow cobblestone lane.

Halfway up the street, a car ahead whipped around a corner and was headed straight for us. Without even looking, my cabbie jerked the car abruptly back over into the right hand lane, wedging us tightly between two cars, nearly hitting both in the process. I'm quite certain the only reason we didn't hit anyone was because the car behind us hit its brakes just in the nick of time. I decided at that moment that buckling my seat belt would be a good move on my part.

As soon as the oncoming car had passed us by, my cabbie, who from here on out I will refer to as Paco, pulled us right back into the opposing lane and continued passing the cars in front of us. A couple of the cars honked their horns as we passed, but Paco paid them little attention. I was pretty drunk, so I was finding the driving experience to be quite amusing. At the same time, I was starting to feel slightly nervous. Maybe the booze was wearing off. Where's a flask of whisky when you need one?

After passing the last of the cars in the lane, we entered an intersection. Paco cranked the wheel hard to the right, cutting off another driver, and narrowly missing and removing the front bumper from his car. More honking of horns ensued behind us as we headed off in a new direction. Onward and upward! May the manic ride continue.

Paco kept up his erratic manoeuvers through the small downtown center, all the way to the freeway. I was being thrown around violently like a sock in the dryer. When we hit the open road, I thought we'd be in for a smoother ride. Boy was I mistaken. Apparently, Paco really took my proposal to heart. Paco had the eye of the tiger!

He must have genuinely thought that the quicker he got me to my hotel, the bigger his tip was going to be. To be honest, at this point I thought about paying him and getting him to drop me off right where we were. But then a sober thought entered my mind and I realized that it probably wasn't the greatest idea for a lone tourist to be dropped off in the middle of nowhere in the wee hours of the morning in Mexico. So we ventured on. I again checked my seatbelt, ensuring that it was cinched up nice and tight.

A moment after merging onto the highway, we flew up hard onto the ass of an unsuspecting vehicle in the left lane of a four lane highway (with two lanes in either direction that were actually painted!). The car in front of us was clipping along at a pretty good rate of speed. As he had already made crystal clear, no one could drive fast enough for Paco.

He decided to pick up where he had left off moments earlier and pulled into the oncoming lane to pass. Now, I wasn't too worried when Paco was driving into oncoming traffic in the city because no one could really drive all that fast on narrow cobblestone lanes. But everyone that shared the paved freeway was driving, more or less, as fast as they could. Whereas an accident in the town would have stung a little, an accident now would likely kill. Needless to say, my nervousness was steadily increasing. I had never driven with Paco before, so I did not trust him. I needed another drink. If only he'd step on it!

So here I was in the backseat of a cab in Mexico, being driven by a man that I was now reasonably convinced was trying to kill me. We were actively driving into oncoming freeway traffic, passing a car that we had been tailgating for a half mile or so, until room permitted for us to pass. A moment later, I looked up and saw that another car was quickly approaching us, head on.

It would seem that Paco was an expert in the game of chicken because he didn't even flinch. With a steady hand, he stayed the course. Helpless, I found myself pressing my right foot hard to the floor as if I had a brake pedal of my own in the backseat. A hundred yards or so before we were set to collide, the oncoming driver conceded and changed lanes to avoid a serious collision. Thank God!

At this point, I was more than a little pissed off with my douchebag chauffeur. Sure, I had told him to be the first to arrive, but I didn't tell him that it was my wish to die in a spectacular vehicular collision.

I decided to speak up and told him that I wasn't really in that big of a rush and that he could slow down. Apparently he no longer understood the English language. He merely smiled at me in the rear-view mirror and continued his erratic driving the entire way back to my hotel. This cab ride had turned into a journey from hell. Was I dreaming? Was this a hallucination? Was it a bad idea to have eaten the worm at the bar? Would I ever see my friends and family again? Do they have Taco Bell in Mexico? Needless to say, a lot of questions were running through my brain.

While I may have been highly inebriated when I first entered the cab, by the time we arrived at the hotel, about twenty frightening minutes later, I was dead sober and in desperate need of some hard liquor to calm my frayed nerves. And bikini clad women. That always helps!

I got out of the cab, paid the man and thanked him for the wonderful experience. Then I turned around, got onto my hands and knees, kissed the ground and then bee lined it to the lobby bar. I promptly ordered a tall shot of tequila, followed by three more. I threw them down my throat so fast I didn't even taste them. It felt good to be alive. Here's to you, Paco, you maniac! Viva Mexico! That man nearly caused about a dozen car accidents while taking me on a demented thrill ride to my hotel. Paco was a monster douchebag for disrespecting my life and the lives of others on the road, but to his credit, he really did put some hurry up into it!

CHAPTER 9

HELLO NEIGHBOUR

I USED TO LIVE in an apartment. The builder actually called it a condo, but I assume that the word condo is just some yuppie way to say apartment. You can rent a condo and you can own a condo. You can rent an apartment and you can own an apartment. Both of them are homes off of common hallways in buildings that usually have stairwells and elevators, so what's the difference? I feel like the difference between a condo and an apartment is the same as the difference between 6:00 p.m. and 1800 hours, but I digress.

Bank On It

I DON'T PAY RENT to a landlord. Instead, I pay it to the bank in the form of a mortgage. Mortgages are complete bullshit. The interest rates fluctuate depending on...well...who the hell really knows. Interest rates are like PMS-ing women, they are unpredictable, to say the least. You could be paying a supposedly low interest rate for a couple of years and then, for no reason whatsoever, some jackass decides on a whim that the economy would be better off if interest rates were increased. Next thing you know it's shot up one percent. And all of this is controlled by one man, as far as I can tell. It is literally one dude's decision as to what to do with interest rates. I've got to say, that seems like a pretty fool proof system.

The concept that paying more money (than I currently do to the bank for my home) will somehow be beneficial to me and the economy is a difficult concept to grasp. Perhaps I lack the mental prowess to understand how going further into debt, how departing with more of my money is a good thing for me and the economy at large. So, even though my wage did not increase and even though the price of everything else around me has gone up substantially, somehow paying a bigger mortgage for my home will benefit me and my fellow humans? Why don't they just bend me over a table and have their way with me, no need to buy me a drink first. Hell, don't even bother with the lube. It's an expense I just can't afford anymore. Spit will do.

Banks are nothing more than the legalized mafia. Sure, they'll loan you money, but you're now indebted to them, big time. Whatever you take from them, you're going to pay back in spades. If you don't pay it back, they'll just take all the shit you 'own' and break your financial legs.

The worst part is that they'll store your hard earned dollars, charge you a fee to safeguard it, and possibly another fee when you make a purchase. Those fees, known as bank fees, are one of the biggest scams perpetrated on the human population. It took an amazing douchebag of a banker to create bank fees. I hope he rots in insolvency for his entire afterlife.

Basically, the bank will hold on to what little money I have, invest it and earn interest. I will receive a very small percentage of that interest in return, provided my money is in a savings account. If it's not, then I receive no interest at all.

They will also use my money to give loans to other customers, loans on which interest is charged to make the bank even more money. I don't see a dime of that either. There would appear to be a common theme when it comes to bank dealings.

At other times, the interest they earn off of my back goes straight into the pockets of the rich bankers that run the show. Those bankers are glorified mobsters who have paid-off politicians in order to have the deck stacked in their favour. They are rich and powerful and they run the world. They have politicians and law-makers in their back pockets and there is nothing we can do about it. Holy hell do I sound like a pot-smoking conspiracy theorist right now! I even looked over both shoulders before writing that last part.

Let's get serious for a second here though: are there no honest politicians left? It's amazing what rich and powerful people can get away with. Maybe I should open my own bank? I'll call it, 'I Get Rich off of the Hard Work of Others National Bank.' At least the name would be honest and forthcoming, because you can be sure as Shaq is tall that absolutely nothing else will be above board.

The true problem is that we can't do anything without banks. Everything runs through them. They've got their fingers into everything, like my children at a wedding buffet dessert table. It's like Michael Corleone has gone legit and now runs a bank. We're all forced to come in and kiss his hand to show our respect.

If you want a house, you go and talk to the bank about it. If you want a car, you go and talk to the bank about it. If you need to renovate your home or your kids need to go to college, you go and talk to the bank about it. Then they make you sweat a little, maybe act like they're not going to give you what you want, but in the end they pull out ten thousand pages for you to sign and take your soul as collateral. Oh, and there's just one other catch: you're going to end up paying back triple what they gave you in the first place. It's a mad world we live in, isn't it? Independent loan sharks are illegal yet banks are legit. Go figure?

If I could live my life without using a bank, I would. But that's the crazy thing, you really can't. You cannot live your life without a bank, that's the way the system works. They've got their tentacles into everything and there's nothing you or I can do about it – unless someone wants to crank *Pixies* and go *Fight Club* on their asses. And for those of you who have no idea what that last sentence means, please go out and buy a Pixies album or two and watch *Fight Club*. Otherwise your man card may be revoked.

Apartment Life

LIVING IN an apartment – or condo – isn't that great. I personally wouldn't recommend it unless you are just too old, too lazy, or don't have the time to look after a house and a yard of your own. Usually people have no choice but to live in an apartment because they cannot afford a decent house.

It isn't always the fact that you can't afford a house that keeps you out of one. There are people who live in cities where, even if they wanted a house, they wouldn't find one. Areas like Paris or Manhattan are just so crowded that the only available residences are apartments. If you want to live in either one of those cities, then you'd better like living in close quarters.

I had never lived in an apartment until a few years ago. Growing up, I had always lived in houses. When I moved out after high school, I rented various basement suites before I rented a house with a few buddies while going to school. But then once I landed a job, I ended up living in an apartment for a handful of years. I didn't like it when I first moved in, and I liked the place even less when I moved out a few years later. It most certainly did not grow on me.

It's not that my apartment wasn't nice, because it was just fine, other than being too small. The main problem is that your neighbours are in far too close a proximity for my liking. You pass them out in the halls, ride the elevators with them and see them in the lobby and the parking garage. You can hear them when they walk past your front door and smell them when the bottle of perfume they've bathed in lingers in the hallway until it finds its way under your front door. If your downstairs neighbour takes a screamer to bed, you hear that too. Good on him, though.

While some neighbours are fine people, others are not. When you live in a neighbourhood of houses, you probably have the same ratio of douchebags that you would in an apartment building. The only difference is that in an apartment the douchebags are right in your face. Instead of being two hundred yards down the street, they are twenty feet from your door.

In an apartment complex, or tenement or what have you, it is very likely to have someone living above, below, to the left, to the right and across the hall from you. You are completely boxed in by other people and that is the crux of the problem. Because of this tight-quartered living, my dislike for people in general grew substantially over the years I lived like that. It grew to a point where I decided to write a book called *Don't Be a Douchebag*. Now that's saying something.

I used to assume that people were good until proven otherwise. However, for the most part, I now assume you're a douchebag until proven innocent. It's easier that way. Apparently I have become a cynical man. I have been ruined by people! I used to smile all of the time, now I only smile when I'm drunk, which is only most of the time.

There were people who treated the hallways like a toilet for their pets, allowing their untrained dogs to urinate and defecate onto the carpets. Worse than that, some of my neighbours couldn't be bothered to clean up after their dogs. They just didn't give a shit. Their dogs, on the other hand, gave lots of shits. It's living in close quarters with these types of people that really made me hate apartment life. Corridor poop will do that to a man.

One thing that helped me keep my sanity was subscribing to the age old adage of tit for tat. If you don't partake in this belief system, I suggest you consider it because it can be a lot of fun.

There was this inbred family who lived at the end of the hall on my floor, about 4 doors down. They always made a tremendous amount of noise outside my door as they came and went. The herd of undisciplined children would stampede up and down the halls like a pack of wild buffalo, tripping to the floor, bumping into walls, and shouting at the tops of their lungs. One little boy, who looked and acted like a serial killer in the making, always seemed to cause his brother to throw full blown temper tantrums outside of my door. Needless to say, I did not enjoy these people. They were as personable as Rain Man and as pleasant as a scratched cornea.

I tried a variety of approaches with these people, although nothing would take. I went out into the hallway to speak with their parents, to explain to them that they are not the only people that live in the building and that, perhaps, they could tone down hallway time. Just turn it down a few decibels. I kindly told them that I didn't appreciate it when their little tyrants would bang on my door as they passed, in an attempt to get my dog to bark. The two youngest of the lot would even stick their tiny fingers under the door, occasionally, to get the dog going. I suggested to the parents that they curb that behaviour, as I was worried that one of their children would one day have a finger find its way into the dog's belly.

But instead of listening to me and, in turn, providing a little discipline to their children, the severely uneducated parents treated me as if I was the asshole in this situation, and chastised me for daring to tell them how to raise their awful children. I bit my lip and did my best to refrain from ripping both of their throats out on the spot. Since there were potential witnesses around, I instead devised a payback plan to be played out at a later date.

Since that awful family was up early in the morning due to their plethora of early rising children, I assumed they would be in bed early as a result. Therefore, I decided to strike at night when they would be most vulnerable. I should say, as a side note, one of the things I find to be most unfortunate in life is that the lower the IQ of a couple, the less likely they are to be sterile. Stupid people breed. And once your brain function dips below a certain threshold, birth control is never mentioned, spoken of or used.

The following weekend, upon getting home at about two in the morning from a drunken night out with my buddies, I took a little detour past my place and over to my favourite inbred neighbours' door.

After placing a small piece of tape over their peep-hole (If you're trying this at home, don't use scotch tape), I began stomping the ground while making obscenely loud and raunchy sex noises. I wasn't stingy with it either. I made it loud and I made it last. Then I banged on their door with the palm of my hand and I made it count! Payback is a bitch!

Needless to say, no one came out to see what the hell was going on – not with that piece of tape I had obstructing their peep-hole. They were probably scared shitless. I'm such an asshole at times. At least that's what my wife tells me. But I justify it to myself by only being an asshole to those who truly deserve it. Those people truly deserved it. That's how I sleep at night. Anyway, I made good and sure I had woken everyone up in that place before I turned and walked back the dozen paces or so to my place for a nightcap. Good luck getting all of your terrible little children back to sleep, you degenerate douchebags. Don't fuck with a motherfucker! I know I may be childish, but that's because I'm still a kid at heart.

CHAPTER 10

IMMIGRATION

MANY IMMIGRANTS are wonderful people, even pillars of society. Arnold Schwarzenegger is an immigrant and he is arguably the greatest man in America. But not all people are created equal. There are a good number of immigrants who are ignorant douchebags. If you've been paying any attention at all to what I've written thus far, it should come as no surprise to you that in this chapter I will be focusing my attention on the latter.

I know that immigration can be a touchy subject for many people, but don't worry, I'll treat the subject with the same amount of sensitivity and sophistication that I've displayed thus far. If you are already getting your panties in a bunch, don't even bother. I love immigrants, just not in my country. I'm sick and tired of all these immigrants coming here and taking all our jobs!

I kid, of course. If I really felt that way, I'd have to write a chapter about myself in this book, because I'd be a prejudiced douchebag. I do love it, though, when I hear of people complaining about immigrants taking jobs away from citizens. Most often the jobs being performed by the immigrants in question are jobs that the home-grown population aren't willing to work. But hell, there I go making sense again, and nobody likes sensibility. Anyway, in case you have severe attention deficit disorder, this chapter is about immigrants.

In North America, well at least the North America that is north of Mexico, almost everyone's families, at one point or another, were immigrants. Canada and the United States were built on immigration and still need immigrants to grow and thrive. My mother was born in Scotland and moved across the pond as an adult. If I were to say that I hated all immigrants I would inherently be stating that I hated my mum. (Mum is how you say mum in Scotland and that's the proper way, my mum would have you know. They say 'mom' in the United States and don't even get me started on how incorrect and horrible sounding that is to a Scottish lady.)

I love my mum. I feel no ill towards her, not in the slightest. Although, my mum may not be too pleased with me after she reads my book. But who am I kidding? She'll never read this book. She's better than that. She raised me to be better than this.

So, while I don't have a problem with all immigrants, what I do have a problem with are… wait for it… douchebag immigrants. You may be thinking to yourself right now, 'What makes an immigrant a douchebag immigrant?' Well, for one, they're not my mum or Arnold Schwarzenegger.

Good immigrants are a relatively self-explanatory group. They come to their new country with the best of intentions. They like their new country and are happy to be there. They enjoy the culture, the people, and the pastimes. They fluently speak the language of their new home or, at the very least, are trying their best to get a firm grip on it. These immigrants either have deep pockets (i.e. money they've brought over from the old country with them) or have gainful employment as to not be a burden to their new society. At the bare minimum, they have a good work ethic and an education.

Good immigrants don't want to cause any problems in their new country. They don't rob their local 7-Elevens, they don't deal drugs to children and they don't steal cars. They go out of their way to try to teach their children how to be good citizens, not criminals. They are the kind of people that you would want to welcome into your country with open arms, plain and simple.

Douchebag immigrants are a whole other entity. To begin with, they don't speak the language of their new country. In my humble opinion, if you do not speak the official language of your new country and have no intention of ever learning it you should never have been allowed to immigrate in the first place. What kind of person wants to move to a new country without desire to learn the local language? A lazy, uncaring burden to society, that's who.

Whenever I'm in a foreign country, I always try to learn as much of that country's language in the short period of time that I am there. Usually it's just a few key words and phrases that I pick up, but it's better than nothing, and I enjoy it. I love languages. I wish I knew every language in the world. I couldn't imagine making a permanent move to a foreign country and not wanting to learn the local language, not doing my best to pick it up as quickly as possible. That's asinine. It's extremely ignorant and shouldn't be tolerated. But unfortunately, it has become a relative norm with regards to immigration.

I have met people who have been living in Canada for longer than I have been alive. Yet they act as if they do not even know what I'm saying if I ask them something as elementary as their name. That's unbelievable! I mean, the ignorance of some people just floors me. It really pisses me off to know that we let these jokers into our country. And not only did we let these douchebags in the door, but our government, in its infinite wisdom, probably told some other really good prospects, prospects that actually spoke English and gave a shit about our country, that they couldn't immigrate because we were over quota on decent human beings and needed to diversify, or some bullshit like that.

An unwillingness to learn the language of your new homeland is but one of the things that makes an immigrant douchebag. Another factor is when you immigrate to your new country and do nothing but break the law from the day you arrive. As if we don't already have enough crime, it appears as if the government goes out of their way to import more criminals.

So, now after the stellar job performed by immigration services, we find ourselves with a brand new immigrant, or even a 'refugee', that has just committed a crime. Perhaps they will go to jail. If so, now the taxpayers are on the hook to provide this douche with a jail cell and three squares a day, not to mention free education and who the hell knows what other perks they get in the slammer. (Prison's not really as great as I'm making it sound. For instance, most would not consider sodomy a perk. I'm just emphasising the excessive amount of tax dollars it costs to keep someone locked up. I've never been, but I'm certain it sucks there.) Now, that really rubs me the wrong way, like the unwanted touch a drunken drag queen on the midnight train. It's not like we couldn't use those tax dollars somewhere else, like to build bigger prisons. In all reality, imported criminals should simply be deported. Plain and simple... and certainly cost effective.

Think about it. Here is a person that has never paid a tax dollar in our country. Out of the goodness of our hearts, we let them come here to live. Then they thank us by shooting a bystander at a nightclub. After a legal trial that eats up a lot of taxpayer cash, they go to jail, which costs even more taxpayer coin. And to grind just a little more salt into the wound, we have to provide a government-paid translator for the douchebag criminal because he hasn't even bothered to learn to speak English.

Now, why the hell should we pay for this ass wipe to reside in our prisons? We should merely ship him home, whether he's become a citizen since arriving or not. There should be a clause in the immigration agreement that states as much. Who cares if he goes to jail or not back in his home country? I don't care if he was a legitimate political refugee. At least he won't be here anymore, committing crimes and costing us money, pain and suffering. Deportation as a punishment for crimes committed would probably be a pretty damn good deterrent. It's certainly worth a shot.

Another thing that irritates me - something that definitely puts the douche into douchebag immigrant - are the people who always say, with every chance they get, how things were better back in the old country.

I have had conversations with people like this before and it drives me crazy. They say things like, 'The food is much better in the old country, the weather is much nicer back home, the people are much friendlier where I come from, the grass is greener, the streets are cleaner, the women are hornier and have bigger tits,' and on and on and on, ad nauseam.

To all of these people I have a simple message: go back home. If everything was so much better where you came from, why the hell did you ever leave in the first place? Go back home, you ungrateful fool. And if it's true what you say about the women, take me with you.

But the ultimate douchebag immigrant, the one who really takes the cake and puts the cherry on top, is the one who wants to blow up his new country – the dude who wants to see it burn. Of all the lousy, no-good things that someone could do to their adoptive country - and I know I'm going out on a big limb here by writing this - destroying it has got to be at the top of the heap.

These explosive douchebags have come here claiming to be refugees, or something of that nature, and our country took them in with open arms. We gave them food, shelter and guidance to get back on their own feet - all because it was apparently too dangerous for them to live in their country of origin. Therefore, out of the kindness of policies, we adopted them so that they wouldn't have to worry about being killed just for minding their own business back from where they came. And how do they return the favour? They return it with a plan to blow up some of their adoptive country's innocent people by means of suicide bombing. Or perhaps a mass shooting is more to their liking. Either way, Allah must be very proud of them. I'm sure that 72 virgins will be waiting for each and every one of them in the afterlife, as promised. The only thing Allah didn't tell them is that they just might be 72 extremely horny, gorilla-like man-virgins with an endless supply of Viagra. Oh, and that they'll be in hell. Enjoy the afterlife, jihadi-douche.

Durka Durka Durka

THIS BRINGS ME to the worst offence of all: the importation of ignorance, racism and discrimination. I'm talking about the fact that our society permits immigrants and refugees to continue to practice and preach things that fly in opposition to the laws, beliefs systems and moral fibre that this beautiful country was based on. Because of our bleeding-heart ways, our government allows certain human rights offences to take place merely because they are afraid that they may offend a certain group of people were they to ban awful practices and behaviours. It's disgraceful. It's distasteful. It's the Canadian way, eh!

As you are probably well aware, a number of Muslim men force their women to wear ridiculous looking full-body suits known as burkas. For those of you who've been living under a rock these past few years, a burka is like a gown - usually black in colour - that covers a woman's entire body. Add to that a veil that covers a woman's face completely, save for a slit for her eyes. I guess the women wearing these sexy little numbers should feel blessed that they are allowed the luxury of vision. They should be grateful that they can breathe through the damn things too. Because these women are possessions, and you can do whatever the hell you want to with your possessions.

The reason behind the hideous getup is so that no other man may look upon your woman, or more precisely, your property. I don't understand it at all. Are the men in those Muslim countries so prone to raping women that they've got to keep all women as covered up as possible? Honestly, these dudes must have absolutely no control over their bodies and actions in the presence of women. That's got to be the case. Their brains must shut down and they must completely lose control if they see so much as a bare naked lady-ankle. Hands and penises just spring to life and ravage uncontrollably. I can't think of any other reason why you'd want to hide your wife and daughters from the general public.

These poor women have to go out every day with bed sheets draped over them from head to toe, even if it's just to pick up a loaf of bread or a carton of milk from the corner store. And I'm willing to bet those aren't five hundred thread count Egyptian cotton sheets either. Rain or shine, even if it's a hundred and twenty degrees out (most do come from the desert), these women are forced to wear a table cloth at all times. They even have to try to eat – if they want to grab a bite while out and about - with a huge sheet of cloth covering their mouths. Personally, I have a hard enough time getting all my food into my mouth at the best of times. I don't need a bed-skirt around my face to make matters more difficult. And it must be super difficult for the ladies of the night, because most johns want to see the goods before they purchase. Burkas must be really bad for business.

As I write this, burkas are banned or beginning to be banned in certain countries around the world. I've got to say I couldn't agree more with that action. May the good Lord above bless those countries for standing up for human rights. It's nice to see a western country finally show some backbone and not bend to all the wishes and wants of every new face that comes to town.

You see, the manner in which tough countries tackle immigration is through assimilation. I know, that sure sounds crazy, doesn't it? Why would we expect anyone to actually try to fit in? The thought process follows that if you want to live in their country, you will act accordingly. You are to follow and abide by their laws and live harmoniously with other citizens. If that doesn't sound like something you're willing to do, then take a hike because they don't want you. Amen.

One of the ways for douchebag immigrants to illustrate that they are not part of their new country is to force their women to look as dramatically different from the rest of society as possible. Wearing a burka makes a woman stand out as much as an obese black man does at an albino anorexia convention.

Obviously, in Western society there is freedom to practice your religion. And just for the record, I have absolutely no problem with non-fanatical Muslims. However, a burka is not part of the Koran. It has nothing to do with religion, contrary to what many ignorant, bleeding-heart westerners assume. It has everything to do with Muslim women's severe lack of human rights. Again, I should specify I'm referring to fanatics, not run of the mill, decent human beings who happen to be Muslim. There are plenty of wonderful, normal, non-misogynistic Muslims out there. Mike Tyson comes to mind. So does Muhammad Ali. Apparently pugilists like to convert. Apparently the vast majority of my knowledge about the world is sports based.

Here's some history for you: In 100 AD, 500 years before Mohamed wrote the Koran, Plutarch, a Greek historian, wrote: 'Most barbarous nations, and the Persians in particular, reveal the harsh and cruel side of their nature in the jealousy with which they behave to their women. Not only their wives, but even their slaves and concubines are closely guarded, so that they are never seen by strangers; at home they are shut up indoors, and when they travel they are carried about under awnings which are surrounded with curtains and placed on four-wheeled wagons.'

In western countries, just in case you were unaware, women and men have equal rights. Actually, women probably have even more rights than men do - or at least they can get away with more if they are good-looking and have nice cleavage on display. Permitting Muslim men to force their women to dress like big, black ghosts, among other things, is an infringement on women's rights and that's bullshit. Damn, I sound like a feminist, don't I? What's wrong with me?

Sure, women may not be able to do certain things as well as men can - like driving cars, throwing balls or growing chest hair, for instance - but that doesn't mean that they shouldn't have the right to do those things, none the less. (Ladies, I anxiously await your hate mail. I'd love to hear from you. Send pictures!)

Again, don't go thinking that I have a problem with all Muslim people. Obviously, as much as I would like to do so, I can't paint everyone with the same brush. For instance, contrary to what my brush has always painted, apparently not all sons of immigrant Scottish mothers are incredibly handsome. Go figure.

You see, I pretty much get along with all people from all walks of life, at least those who do not wear egregious hatred, bigotry and racism on their sleeves. I mean, minor hatred, bigotry and racism I can handle, but I just can't roll with egregious. That's just who I am.

As I am well aware, there are plenty of Muslim immigrants out there who do assimilate, who do learn their adoptive country's language and who do not supress their women or display misogynistic behaviour. These people should be welcomed as openly as any other immigrants, especially if they come from a country with excellent cuisine.

My main problem is the double standard. If, when in your Muslim country, I am forced to abide by all the rules and regulations of that country, as ignorant and undemocratic as they may be to me, why then, when fanatical Muslims come here, are they able to demand to have all of the same rights they had in their messed up home country, as ignorant and undemocratic as they me be?

We need to stop being such pathetic pushovers in the West. We need to stop bending to the will of every douchebag immigrant we import into the country. If you want to come here you have to play nice and get along with everybody else. It's like kindergarten. As long as you keep your hands to yourself and don't piss your pants too often, everything should be just fine. If that doesn't sound agreeable, don't come here. Cut and dry. I should run the world. You wish!

Peace

SINCE I HAVE SHARED some strong, and quite possibly drunkenly ignorant, opinions over the last few paragraphs, I'm going to now use what is referred to as the 'sandwich technique'. This is a technique that can be used when criticizing somebody that you don't want to offend. I use this with my wife all the time and it goes a little something like this: 'Honey, your hair looks so beautiful today. You know, when you yell at me incessantly for absolutely no reason whatsoever it makes me want to bail out and start a new life on my own in Mexico. Have your tits gotten bigger?'

So here we go: Overall, I like immigrants. Like I previously wrote, my mother came here years ago and if she hadn't, I wouldn't be here today writing this modern-day masterpiece. But certain immigrants need to smarten up, learn the language, and ditch the hatred. I especially like immigrants if for no other reason than that they provide us with a massive variety of great foods and restaurants. I love to eat, and life would be so mundane without the diversity I have to choose from because of people moving to my country from all over the world. So thank you for that, immigrant population. Thank you for spicing up my life. Although, my colon, at times, has mixed feelings about you, especially the morning after an exotic feast.

CHAPTER 11

NO ENGLISH

AT THIS POINT in the book, you may be getting the impression that I have a strong dislike of certain types of people in the world. I would like to take this opportunity to clarify my stance. I dislike all people, equally. I do not focus my displeasure of people to include only certain groups or aspects of society.

Instead, I let my disdain for people cover a broad aspect of the world. I don't think it can be called discrimination if you discriminate against all people equally, and that is exactly what I do.

If I think you're a moron, I'll call you a moron. If I think you're a douchebag, I'll call you a douchebag. If I think you have nice tits, I'll just keep that thought to myself. But here's the thing, it doesn't matter who you are, where you come from or what you look like, if I don't like you, then I don't like you. It's that easy. I just thought I'd share my Zen-like stance with you all. Please enjoy the non-discriminatory words that follow.

I've encountered many of these people in the past and will confront them again in the future. There is no doubt in my mind that you have come across them as well. They may live down the block from you or in the same apartment building. To make a long story short, they appear to have absolutely no troubles at all getting by in life.

They drive a car and therefore must have a driver's licence. They have school-aged kids that attend local public schools and they shop in the same grocery stores that you do. It would appear, for all intents and purposes, that they function in society just as any other person does. But the difference between them and you is that when they do something offside, such as blatantly cut you off with their car in the strip-mall parking lot, once confronted, they pretend that they do not speak English.

While coming alarmingly close to destroying your vehicle in a well-executed attempt at stealing a parking spot right out from under you, the moron parks his car, pretending as if he didn't even notice you and your vehicle. Then, when you roll down your window and holler your disapproval his way, he responds by saying something like, 'Uhh, no English… I no understanda.'

Apparently this dude spoke English when he took his driver's license exam. One would assume that he spoke English with the salesman that sold the man his car. I would also presume that the guy would not have successfully interviewed for his job without speaking English. I'm also quite confident that he would not understand any of the street signs on the road if he didn't speak or read English, although that may actually explain a thing or two.

What I'm trying to say is that I'm pretty damn sure that the douche-bag speaks English. But because this loser pulled a dirt bag manoeuvre and is afraid of confrontation, he now conveniently does not speak English and therefore does not know, or at least cannot be made to understand, what it is that he has done wrong. No matter what you may say to him at this point, he will look at you with a very confused look on his face, periodically interjecting his favourite phrase, 'No English.'

I live in the Vancouver area and that means that immigrants are everywhere. The city is referred to as a melting pot of cultures. I like melting pots. I know I've said it before, but melting pots bring great foods.

Whatever I might be in the mood for from whatever country I can think of, there will be a restaurant somewhere relatively nearby that serves it. For instance, I just saw a show on TV about Malaysia and wondered to myself what kind of food they eat. Instead of going all the way to the Orient - which would be fun but not very cost or time effective - all I have to do is travel a few blocks or miles and I will be able to find a Malaysian restaurant somewhere, I'm sure.

The point I'm trying to make here is that I don't hate all people who come from different countries, and I don't hold a grudge against all people who don't speak English. But I do dislike those people who can speak English but refuse to speak it in order to try to get out of a predicament or to justify douchebag behaviour. The 'No English' cared permits these people to be chronic assholes. If you speak the language, speak it. Don't use it when it is convenient for you, only to then forget it when you want to pretend as if you don't understand how your behaviour makes you a massive dickhead.

No Subtitles Needed

As you are aware, I am not a big fan of apartment living. I do not enjoy being in close proximity to such a large number of people, especially those who I feel are detriments to society or just plain horrible human beings.

One of these delightful people to whom I am referring was a woman who lived on the same floor as I did for roughly three years. This woman was Korean and, from what I could tell, lived in an apartment with at least three generations of her family. She was of the middle-ish generation.

I would see her and her family over the years in the hallway or the lobby and I would often smile and nod at them or say 'Hello.' Oddly enough, I never saw a man with them. There were only women and children. Even more strange was that I never once received even the slightest neighbourly gesture in return. All I ever got from any of them were blank stares. Maybe when people smile and nod at you in Korean culture it means something else, something negative and derogatory – I don't know. So maybe they thought that I was a rude asshole for smiling at them.

After living in the building for a year or two, this woman got herself a dog. It was a tiny little snow white powder-puff dog that I'm pretty sure ran on triple-A batteries. It couldn't have been any more than three pounds soaking wet with a brain the size of the average Kardashian.

Now, some people say that there are no bad dogs rather there are merely bad dog owners. I'm going to say it right here: that woman was a remarkably awful dog owner.

Beginning the day she got her dog, from time to time there would be little puppy poops left in random places around the building. Was it merely a coincidence? I don't think so. That would be too coincidental. Sometimes a little turd would be found in the front lobby. Sometimes there would be a nice little doggy doo waiting to be stepped on immediately outside the front doors of the building.

Other times there might be a little fermenting doggy doo left in the elevator or on the floor directly outside of the elevator. Surprise! And that is just the visible shits that I saw. Only the Lord almighty knows how many times that dog went number one around the place, pissing on the tile floors or on the hallway carpets without anyone but its douchebag owner in the know. It was really nice to see that this woman considered the entire building to be nothing more than a toilet for her lovely little doggy. Her dog treated the apartment building in the same fashion that Donald Trump does human beings, or Mexicans, or Mexican human beings, or anyone who is not Donald Trump.

Some of my neighbours, at least the ones who were actually willing to have conversations, also knew who the culprit of these periodical surprises was, but none of us could ever do anything about it, as we had never caught the perpetrator, with its owner, in the act. That was until the day that I caught them in the act.

I was leaving for work, and as I shut my door and turned the deadbolt, a motion to my left caught my attention. When I turned to see what it was, I was so delighted and pleased to see little Fluffy, right in the middle of the hallway, taking a good, long piss on the carpet. The dog was a mere two or three paces from my front door. Little Snowflake's mentally deficient owner was standing by with her back turned to the dog as it urinated indoors. She was doing her best to pretend not to notice what was happening. Being the courteous man that I am when confronted by degenerate douchebag behaviour, I immediately shouted, 'Hey, your dog's pissing on the carpet!'

When I spoke, she turned to face me. The dog was still relieving itself onto the floor. With a confused look on her face, she said to me, 'Huh?' So I pointed, with my finger of course, down to the little princess and said to her again, 'Your dog is peeing on the carpet!'

Looking down at her dog and clearly seeing that it was actively voiding its bladder, she looked back up to me and again, with a confused look on her face repeated the phrase 'Huh?'

At this point, she was very lucky that she was not a man because I probably would have slapped her to the ground. I was stunned by her blatant ignorance. The battle had begun. It was on! I was going to break her!

Standing there, staring at her now with fire in my eyes, I said to her, 'Are you fucking with me?'

Instead of doing what it was that I really wanted to do to her (which would most likely have landed me an assault charge), I decided to try to continue speaking to her.

'Are you fucking kidding me? Can you really not see what is happening right before your very eyes? Can you even see me? Am I here right now? Is your dog's urination merely an illusion? Are you a street magician? Can you levitate? When are you going to clean up your dog's mess?'

All she did was look at me with a constipated look on her face. Then she finally spoke, and in a high pitched voice that sounded like her vocal cords were crushing a baby chipmunk she said, 'Ah ha ha, no English.'

Pow! There it was, the immigrant trump card of 'No English.' It was superbly executed, I must say, but this was far from my first rodeo, let me tell you.

I had already lived in the Vancouver area for a few years at that point in life and was all too familiar with many people's frequent use of the phrase 'No English.' So when the owner of that lovely little dog gave me the immigrant douchebag catch-phrase, I responded by calling her bluff. I told her that I knew that she had been living in the building for as long as I had been, which was nearly three years at the time, and followed that up by telling her that I knew that she spoke English.

Upon being bombarded by all of my English vocabulary, I could tell she was starting to get rattled. To her credit though, she stuck to her guns and this time said, 'Uh, I no undestanda.'

So I told her again that I knew that she was lying about not being able to speak English. I repeated to her that I knew how long she had been living in the building. Then I said to her that if she truly couldn't speak a word of English after living in Canada for at least three years, the only explanation must be that she was mentally retarded. So I asked her if she was allowed to be out in the hallway, unsupervised without her caregiver.

Now, I knew that she had understood what I had said, because instead of again saying something like, 'No English,' this time she stomped her feet while standing in place and swung her arms awkwardly as if she were a little girl on the cusp of a temper tantrum. Maybe she was intellectually disabled after all? Was I picking on a mentally handicapped lady? Oh well, it was too late for me to stop now.

Since I rarely get angry and don't really have much of a temper to speak of, at the sight of the little temper tantrum this lady was throwing, my anger had begun to transform into amusement. I could not believe the fashion in which this woman was reacting to me and to my accusation that she did, in fact, speak my language. Instead of simply admitting defeat and agreeing to clean up the dog pee, she was playing hardball in the most unusual of ways.

This woman, unfortunately, had no way of knowing what she was getting herself into. If I see I've hit a nerve and that I can easily push your buttons, I become like a shark in blood-filled waters. I love pushing people's buttons, and if you piss me off like she had, then I will stop at nothing until I have broken you down and destroyed you. Holy shit do I have a tendency for hyperbole.

I concluded by asking her how she could watch her dog urinate onto the floor but not be capable of comprehending what it was that the dog was doing. I asked her how she could not understand that I would perceive her behaviour as being extremely strange and unacceptable.

For, apparently, having no knowledge of what it was that I was saying, she sure got angry when I said that last part. She stomped her way over to the elevator and pressed the call button. The elevator door opened immediately. She then stomped her way inside the elevator to escape, but unfortunately for her, the little dog had decided that it would rather stay beside me (I'm sure dogs must know when their owner is a moron and the little mutt decided it would rather be with me. Maybe the dog wasn't so bad after all. Like I said, there are no bad dogs…).

After a few seconds, the elevator door started to close, so the woman, in a panic, blocked it with her arm. She began frantically calling to the dog, calling in vain to get it to come to her. The dog was, of course, not coming because it had clearly never been trained a day in its life, so how would it know what the hell its douchebag of an owner wanted it to do?

Just to give you some insight into the logistics of the situation, the elevators in my building would get angry when the doors were blocked open for more than a few seconds. They would begin sounding an alarm, and then very slowly the doors would force shut, even with the resistance of an arm or a leg attempting to block them open. Therefore, my Korean neighbour was now in a full-fledged panic because the door was being slowly shut on her while her dog was bouncing beside me, trying to play.

Then suddenly, in what I can only describe as a full-on fit of retard rage, the woman threw her keys from inside the elevator out onto the hallway floor, with all the coordination of a non-athletic five year old. A moment or two later, my clearly distraught neighbour clued in to what she had just done as the elevator doors were about to shut her inside, and she began to fight and flail her way past the ever-closing and ever-alarming elevator doors and back out into the hallway.

By that point, I had stopped berating the woman with comments and sarcastic put-downs - such as how I wished that more animals would defecate on the carpet outside of my apartment as I so loved the scent. I was now merely standing in the hallway outside of my front door, watching this woman have a total and complete meltdown. It was glorious!

I've got to say that I truly enjoyed it. I mean, this woman had pissed off a lot of people on many an occasion by leaving the dog turds behind for bystanders to step on, slip in, or just to see, smell and try to avoid. And that's just what she was responsible for in our building. Who knows what kind of a piece of human garbage she was elsewhere in everyday life. So, needless to say, I was taking great joy in the fact that I had so fully and completely sent this lady douchebag off the deep end. And all I had to do was speak a few sentences to her in English. I didn't even have to work for it.

Standing there, with a huge grin on my face and in awe of the strange situation, I watched as the now fully hysterical woman pounded her feet to the floor as she made her way off down the hallway. She was now marching away from the once alarming elevator and towards her apartment. I guess she had given up on whatever it was she was going out to do in the first place. That's probably because she was on her way outside to take her dog for a pee, but now that the dog had pissed all over the carpet it really didn't need to go out anymore.

Clearly my presence was making her upset, so I didn't go anywhere. This was payback for her being such a shitty neighbour over the years. Payback was awesome and came easy that day, just how I like it. By now, I had started laughing aloud at the absurd behaviour on display by this crazy woman.

The thing is, in her hysterical state, the woman had clearly forgotten that not only had she thrown her keys to the floor (again, what the fuck was she thinking with that maneuver?) but she had also left her dog behind. The wee canine was still bouncing around beside me, insistent on coercing me to play with it. Court was still out on the dog, so I just let it be.

Halfway down the long hallway, she finally realized that she was forgetting something and was forced to turn around to come back and retrieve it. She was clearly not impressed at the prospect of having to spend yet another second in my presence. I was basking in the absurdity of the situation.

As she approached, she kept calling, frantically, for her dog to come to her. (Amazingly, even though I didn't speak Korean, I still understood what she was trying to do. Go figure.). The dog would not budge from my side. The little dog was clearly hoping that her owner would forget about it and that the mutt could come and live with me. It knew that I was way cooler than its crazy bitch of an owner. Little Snowball was starting to grow on me.

My lovely neighbour had to walk right up to the dog to retrieve it. It wouldn't so much as take a step towards her. As quickly as she bent over and picked little Snowball up from the floor, she flipped herself around and once again took off down the hallway, smashing her feet to the ground and awkwardly flailing her body and bobbing her head while continuing on with her crazy emotional meltdown.

Walking, yet again, straight past her downed keys, I burst out laughing. I couldn't help it. She had forgotten them not once but twice. For a brief second, I thought to myself that I should tell her that she had forgotten her keys, but I was having too much fun. I didn't want the show to end.

It wasn't until she was nearly to the end of the hallway that she realized she had also forgotten her keys. She was furiously pissed off. I was seriously amused.

By the end of this confrontation I was no longer fuming inside. Instead, I was full of joy. At first, I really wanted to forcibly make the woman lick up the pee from the floor and then take her dog to the SPCA where it would have been in much more capable hands. But the mental breakdown that I so easily gave her provided me with all the retribution I needed.

Feeling like I had achieved victory, I pushed the elevator call button to summon my transportation to the parking garage. The woman, her dog, and the rest of her family all moved out the following month. I've been told by my wife that the inconsiderate woman's encounter with me probably had absolutely nothing to do with her extrication from the building, but I like to take full responsibility. I only wish that I could have seen her one last time to send her on her way and wish her the best of luck in the future by uttering to her the iconic phrase, 'No English.'

CHAPTER 12

POLITICALLY INEPT

I COULD MAKE this chapter quite brief by stating that politicians are nothing but a bunch of over-paid, self-indulgent douchebags who are far more prone to serving number one as they are to serving the public. The problem is I'm relatively certain that there are at least a couple odd ones out there whom are good and decent public servants. It wouldn't be too much fun to discuss the mythical creature (or unicorn, if you will) that is a good, honest and selfless politician, so let's focus on the other ninety-nine percent of them that are utterly useless douchebags.

Forrest Gump Made Better Decisions and He Was Half-Retarded

ALL YOU HAVE TO DO is turn on the news at dinner time and you'll hear of some bone-headed political move in the first five minutes of the broadcast. Perhaps it's yet another school or hospital closure. Perhaps the politicians have voted themselves yet another substantial salary raise while simultaneously cutting back the salaries of all essential service employees of cutting their staffing numbers. Maybe the government has made the decision to send some more troops off to yet another war that really doesn't concern anyone in the western hemisphere. The possibilities are limitless. No matter the day, no matter the time, there will be a political move or decision that just makes you shake your head in absolute disbelief. Sometimes it makes me wonder why we don't just revolt and overthrow these gutless morons.

Part of me has debated trying my own hand at politics. That would be the egomaniacal, self-centered, conscienceless part of me. I'm not going to bamboozle you with some pompous and self-righteous reason for considering entering the political field. I considered trying my hand at it for all the wrong reasons, those being the perks that come with the job. The high salaries, the greatest pensions in the land, and the fact that you only 'work' a few months of the year are all very attractive to most any human being struggling through the day to day grind. Aside from those wonderful job perks, it was the obscene expense accounts that all politicians seem to be granted that really caught my eye.

Breakfast, lunch and dinner, all on the taxpayer's dime, and I'm not talking fast food here, I'm talking top-notch restaurants, the kind that have chefs with tall white hats and French accents and absurdly expensive, foreign wine lists. I'm talking about the kinds of restaurants that have servers that call you sir even when you are much younger than they are. And the expense account is not just for you and you alone. You can take all your friends out as often as you like and flip the bill as there would appear to be absolutely no consequence to this behaviour. Thank you, taxpayers!

The perks don't stop there though, not even close. How about first-class flights to wherever in the country you call home, as often as you want to fly, and nights spent in five-star hotels, again all out of the taxpayer's pocket. Fantastic vacations are also part of it, don't fool yourself. They just have to be under some sort of political guise. As long as a brief meeting is arranged with another politician, it's all gravy. In all, it really adds up.

But honestly, I don't think I could ever actually run for politics. I would feel like a real piece of trash claiming a yearly expense account greater than the yearly incomes of all but the upper one percent of my constituents. I mean really, what kind of piece of steaming human excrement does this to the taxpayers he or she is supposed to be fairly representing? Like a rapist to his victim, these politicians take without remorse.

There was a federal politician near my home riding who had an expense account of somewhere in the neighbourhood of six hundred and fifty thousand dollars. You're probably scratching your head right now thinking that's a typo. It's no typo. That's a six, followed by a five, followed by four zeroes. Six hundred and fifty thousand dollars! And that was just his expenses for one year. His salary was somewhere approaching another hundred and fifty thousand dollars on top of that. In this time of excessive cutbacks and layoffs, pay-cuts and lost pensions, it's sickening that such an outrage is allowed to take place by the very people who are supposed to be looking after the best interests and intentions of the public. These are our public servants and they are robbing us blind. We are being anally fisted, against our wills and without lubrication, whether we realize it or not by pompous, self-righteous douchebags.

Now, if you're of the same mind as I, you are probably trying to wrap your head around that staggeringly large figure of an expense account. You are trying to understand how one mere man's expense account could bill for such a large sum of money.

Well, one of the things that this man liked to do with tax payer money was to bill for frequent flights to and from his home which was on the other side of the country. Never throughout the entire year did he take a flight in the economy class. They were all first or business-class. And they were not just flights for him either, but dozens of them were for his family of four.

What a first-class asshole! He is a prime cut, grade-A douchebag. The trouble is, there are more where he came from, plenty more. One of this man's colleagues was, more or less, praised when all the information came out about the gross over-spending of politicians, because he had a much smaller expense account, one of a mere two hundred and fifty thousand dollars.

What the fuck? Again, this information staggered me, like a left hook to the jaw. The fact that a politician was being praised for having spent *only* two hundred and fifty thousand dollars above and beyond his base salary, on such things as flights, meals and hotel rooms, was hard for me to swallow.

I feel like I'm the only nut in the nuthouse. How is it acceptable that one lowly politician can bill for yearly expenditures above and beyond his salary to the sum of a quarter of a million dollars and it be considered not only perfectly acceptable, but praise worthy? These politicians should be imprisoned, not admired. Every single Crown corporation is cutting salaries, benefits, services, and everything else they can possibly cut, yet these douchebags are spending hundreds of thousands of tax dollars, in addition to their over-inflated salaries, on luxuries. Why are they not criminally charged and thrown in prison? I think that would be a fair place to start.

Think about it for a moment. How many 'Average Joe's' income tax totals would you need to pay for just the one politician's (acceptably low) expense account of a quarter million dollars? Well, let's just say for the equation that the average full time salary is fifty thousand dollars a year (I believe it is actually lower than this most places in Canada and the USA) and that the average person pays about twenty percent income tax. That would mean that in order for us taxpayers to cover the wonderful politician's lowly quarter million-dollar a year expense account, it would take a full year's worth of income tax from twenty-five average taxpayers.

Therefore, just for this one politician to eat at fancy restaurants, wine and dine his buddies and fly his family first class throughout the year, one hundred percent of the income tax paid by twenty five average income earners was needed. And for the politician who racked up the six hundred and fifty thousand dollar expense account, it would take sixty-five Average Joe's to foot the bill. That's mental!

Not one cent of those people's income tax went to schools, roads or hospitals, but strictly into one politician's comfort and enjoyment. That is obscene and we must put a stop to this bullshit. We must start demanding accountability from our politicians. We must demand that the expense records (all of them), be made public. These people are elected to serve us, not to loot us.

For all that the politicians do to us, I might as well walk into a Turkish bathhouse with nothing on but ass-less leather chaps and a ball gag. That way I'd still get raped, but at least it wouldn't cost me so damn much money.

Hidden Agendas

WHAT MAKES a politician a true politician? Is it an undeniable need to help society? Is it a come-hell-or-high-water determination to fix social injustices? In most cases, sadly, I'd say no. Basically, a politician isn't a true politician unless he has some sort of hidden agenda. Much like my wife every time she convinces me to go shopping: she may tell me that we're just heading to the mall quickly to get a pair of shoes for my son, and then next thing you know I've been dragged through twenty different stores and have dropped hundreds of dollars more than I was lead to believe I would and have spent two more hours shopping than I was promised. Wow, that was a big segue.

Sure, your local political representative may have been elected because he swore up and down that he would put more money into your children's schools and cut your taxes. More for less always sounds great. Certainly talk like that sounds appealing to the masses. But the reality of the situation, the true reason he wants to be in power, is so that he can help himself, as well as his new-found business buddies, to the pot of gold at the end of the rainbow. He wants to live the true capitalist dream. Truthfully, all my disdain is just jealousy, but I'll go on.

Perhaps you are curious as to how you can use your political power to make yourself richer? You merely cut through the red tape. And how do you do that? The easiest way is to legislate your way around it.

Perhaps no other example of this behaviour shines brighter than that which was displayed by Dick Cheney. In case you have been living under a rock for the past decade or two – or in case you are just too enamoured with celebrity gossip talk-shows to know what's been going on in the real world, let me tell you about Dick Cheney. He is an evil robot disguised as a bald, harmless-looking old man named Dick. He runs on batteries and that is no word of a lie.

Aside from being some sort of half-man, half-machine, Dick Cheney also happens to be, perhaps, the world's biggest douchebag. He corrupted a government and was a prominent figure responsible for turning the United States of America into the obscene mess of a country that it is today. (If I happen to mysteriously disappear after the release of this book, please have the authorities check the torture dungeon in Cheney's basement. We all know he's got one down there. But be quick about it. I don't know how long I would be able to withstand the waterboarding.)

Dick Cheney was a key figure in changing legislation regarding environmental regulations for oil and gas companies. His implementations allowed these companies to no longer be held accountable to prior environmental regulations and laws. These are the same regulations that all other companies and citizens have to abide by. Cheney, therefore, made it legal for the big oil and gas companies to pollute as much as they wanted to, anywhere they wanted to, without any ramifications or consequences for major environmental offences. It was made legal for them to pollute at will. Nice work, Cheney and friends. That's a job well done! Your grandchildren won't have any clean air to breathe or water to drink, but at least you got to piss everyday into a solid gold toilet and brush your teeth with rare Bordeaux.

What that meant in the big picture was that these wealthy oil and gas companies could practice environmentally irresponsible and unsafe procedures in order to cut corners to increase production and profits. There are no words in the English language that are powerful enough to describe their awfulness.

The absence of regulations allowed big and powerful companies to drastically reduce the time, but most importantly the money, spent on the pointless task of keeping the Earth clean from toxins, pollutants and chemicals. After the removal of any and all environmental regulations, bad things started happening to the people, animals, rivers, lakes, oceans, farms and lands around oil and gas production sites. No big deal.

Many land and water ways quickly became polluted, sometimes to the point of causing sicknesses, cancers, mutations and death in people and animals found anywhere near the job or dumping sites. Regardless, the big companies remained above the law. They were not, at any point, held subject to any environmental laws whatsoever. They were essentially enabled to do whatever they so pleased while throwing caution to the wind and gobs of money directly into their bank accounts. They poisoned water and made people and animals sick or dead. But they made bigger profits than they'd ever made otherwise and that's all that really mattered in the end. Oh, and Cheney got rich too. I'd say that Cheney will burn in hell, but hell, he's probably in charge of that place too.

So, what did Cheney have to do with any of this, you may be asking? Well, Cheney was vice president of the United States of America as well as a prominent member of Halliburton, a major player in oil and gas (and probably other deep dark shit I don't even dare dream about). So by using his political power to bend or remove the laws to allow these companies to ruin the environment for the sole purpose of maximizing profits, his bank account grew substantially. Oh, and so did that of all his buddies. He used his political position and power to make him and his cronies even richer than they already were. To call him a douchebag feels like such an understatement. It feels as unworthy a word to describe him as handsome or humble does for me.

This was, however, nowhere near the end of the corrupt reach of Cheney. He had also become a major player in an arms and weapons manufacturing company and, of course, wanted it to prosper at any cost. So he decided to doctor intelligence from the CIA regarding Iraq possessing nuclear weapons, and, more or less, single-handedly started a war just so that he could sell his weapons to the army and make a killing (double entendre intended).

There's no need for me to go into any more detail here. I think I've made my point and I've probably laid my life on the line in doing so. I am a self-righteous idiot. If I wasn't stinking drunk right now I'd probably be a little nervous about what I've just written. God bless liquor!

Dick Cheney is a douchebag. Nay, he is so much more than a douchebag. Anyone who uses their power to perpetrate pure evil merely to make some cash is in a douchebag class all onto himself.

Not all politicians are self-serving assholes. Some don't really care about money and others are already rich enough and don't feel the need to screw anyone over to make even more money. Politicians such as Bernie Sanders and Arnold Schwarzenegger come to mind. They genuinely think that they can make the world a better place, and try their best to do so without unnecessarily harming others.

But there are plenty of politicians out there with the morals of Caligula and the backbones of jellyfish. And just when you let your guard down and begin to lay your trust in them, they will sell you out and nail you to the cross. Or maybe they'll just give you a sucker punch and lift your wallet before you come to.

CHAPTER 13

BORDERLINE

I LIVE ON the West Coast of Canada, close to the 49th parallel. Since the border is so close, it should be convenient for me to cross and go south. Century Link field (where the Seattle Seahawks play) is only about a couple hours' drive away, and the outlet malls that my wife and her friends love are even closer.

But crossing the border isn't always as easy as I think it should be. The biggest problem with entering the United States is dealing with border guards. Now, I have encountered a handful of nice and friendly border guards over the years, but I'm afraid the good and decent ones are few and far between, at least as far as my experiences have gone.

For the most part, it would appear that border guards are chosen strictly for their severe lack of interpersonal skills, not to mention their short tempers and their inability to smile at even the funniest of jokes. Many of the biggest assholes in the world are recruited by the border services, of that I am certain.

While I have no evidence to back me up, I'm sure that on the application form to become a border guard there is a question that is worded something like this: 'On a scale from one to ten, one being the lowest and ten being the highest, how big of an asshole are you?' I guarantee that anyone who marks a nine or less doesn't even get considered for the job.

Most border guards are incapable, I believe, of showing any real human emotion. It's as if they are all a bunch of robots. They are unable to smile, converse, or understand humour. They take pride in being massive dickheads. Their faces do not smile or frown but merely have an emotionless, soulless look to them that immediately lets anyone crossing the border know that they mean business.

The Rubber Glove Treatment

A LITTLE WHILE BACK, just before my first book, *Let Me Put My Poems In You,* was released, I took a trip across the border. My publisher was in Europe at the time and we needed to get some review copies of my book out to the masses. So he shipped several copies of my work of pure genius to Blaine, Washington, which is about a thirty-minute drive from my place in Canada.

Blaine is literally a stone's throw from the border. I'm not kidding. A major league outfielder could throw a ball from the border crossing and hit the Chevron station in Blaine, it's that close. That may be a slight exaggeration. Bo Jackson may be the only man who could achieve such a feat.

So I took a drive across the border. I had a bunch of envelopes in my truck, each stuffed with a letter from my publisher addressed to the various lucky recipients of my book. We were sending copies of *Let Me Put My Poems In You* out to magazines, newspapers and TV shows. Therefore, all I had in the truck with me was several unsealed envelopes with letters inside. I did not have any merchandise at all. Hell, there wasn't even postage on the envelopes because I was heading directly to the Post Office after picking up the parcel of my books from a courier.

Anyway, here I was in my truck, with nothing of any value to anyone in my possession, about to cross the border into the United States of America. I should mention that I had a Nexus card on me as well, which means that I had already been finger printed and had a background check performed – I'll await your letters, conspiracy-theorists – so I didn't expect to have any trouble at all getting across the line.

As I pulled up to the seated border guard, I was greeted with a deadpan stare. He looked at me like he wished he had never been born, or maybe more appropriately, like he was about to make me wish I had never been born.

I stopped my truck and rolled down my window. As he looked off into the distance, the border guard asked me for my passport. I said something to him like 'how's your day going?' He slowly turned his head toward me, a blank stare on his face, and uttered absolutely no response at all. I wanted to get out of my truck right then and there and slap him in the face, but my better judgement took over. I hate it when that happens.

After a few long moments of silence, the border guard asked me where I was going. I pointed up the hill and told him that I was going to Blaine. He then asked me what the purpose of my travel was and I told him that I had some review copies of my book to pick up and mail out at the Post Office.

Maintaining a face without a trace of actual human emotion, he looked me up and down, slowly. I was waiting for him to hand me back my passport, but he just stood there, silent and emotionlessly staring at me for what felt like a small eternity. Finally, he broke the silence by saying, 'It looks like you've just won yourself a random search.' He literally said that. And then a tiny little smile cracked his face. Fucking prick.

The dipshit then informed me that I had to pull my truck around to the side of the building and park it. Then I had to go inside to talk to another border guard.

I was immediately angered. No other emotion would have been appropriate. The search was clearly about as random as an obsessive compulsive's morning routine. And what pissed me off even more was that the bastard actually cracked a smile while he said it. Serenity now!

What a crock of shit. A random search, my ass! If it was really a random search, wouldn't he have told me right from the start that I was going to be getting this random search? Instead, he told me after talking to me for a minute or two and after deciding that he liked me even less than the previous few people that drove through his kiosk, probably because I tried to be sociable with him. That's what you get for trying to be friendly with a border guard.

I, therefore, had no option but to pull my truck around into the complex and park it. Amazingly, as I pulled up to my next stop, the border guard who was directing on me where to park my truck immediately presented himself as an even bigger douchebag than the first idiot I had the displeasure of dealing with.

This border guard was also much bigger and fatter and he looked like he was shy a chromosome or two. I have no doubt that his name must have been something like John-boy or Jim-Bob. He may have been working in the Pacific Northwest, but his roots were clearly from hill-billy bumfucker land in the deep, deep South. I'm talking so deep that kissing cousins are so far apart in blood relation that their relationships are almost frowned upon.

As I parked my truck and shut off the engine, my window was rolled down so that Jim-Bob could speak to me. He barked at me: 'Get out and leave your keys on the hood!'

This whole process was brand new to me. I had never before been subjected to a search. Slightly confused, I asked him 'Do you mean to leave my keys on the dash or literally on the hood?' to which he replied with a sharp and snappy tone, 'What did I say? On the hood.' Okay thanks, you hillbilly bumfucker.

As I stepped down out of my truck, I asked Jim-Bob or Cletus or whatever the hell his name was, if I could take my letters in with me. Staring at me for a few moments with a blank and expressionless look on his face (this must also be part of the job requirement) he finally replied to me by saying, 'I don't know.'

Well thanks for being so helpful! You were oh-so clear about me leaving my keys specifically on the hood of my vehicle, but now you're not sure as to whether or not I can bring my belongings, that I don't want you to ruin and disorganize with your filthy sausage-like fingers, inside with me.

So I asked him again if I could bring my things in with me and this time he told me to leave everything behind. I was told very sternly that I couldn't bring anything in with me. Then I asked him what they were planning on doing to my truck and if they were going to mess with my letters. He told me again, but this time with pure hatred in his voice, to go inside. Not wanting to get shot by some trigger-happy, inbred hill-billy, I did as he instructed.

Once I arrived inside the building, it appeared as if I had just walked into a very large bank. There were several wickets along one wall, some of them empty, the others manned by border guards. There was also one of those rope mazes they like to use in banks to herd people into long, zigzagging lines.

There were not many people waiting in line when I entered and for that I was thankful. I became especially thankful of that fact about five minutes later, when no less than fifty Chinese people filed into line behind me. I wondered to myself if it was some sort of human smuggling ring that had just been caught trying to sneak across the border. More than likely they were just a tour group.

After waiting my turn in line, I approached the next available border guard. This guy was not putting out near the same douchebag vibe as the previous two had been, but we had just met so the court was still out. I was now operating on the guilty until proven innocent principle while dealing with these moronic border guards.

Once I got up to the counter, he asked me why I was entering the United States. I told him about the review copies of my book that I was picking up in Blaine and mailing out. Satisfied with my explanation, he told me to have a seat while he went outside to search my truck. I looked around and there were no seats to be found. I was not surprised. Was that border guard humour, perhaps? There was a large concrete ledge near the window, however. That would suffice.

About ten minutes later, he came back inside with my keys in his hand. It could have been a long ten minutes of waiting, I suppose, but I was thoroughly entertained the whole while by the extremely difficult and awkward conversations that a couple of the border guards were having with some of the Chinese people.

Many of the Chinese group members were speaking varying degrees of broken English with the border guards they were dealing with. That was, until they were asked questions that they didn't want to answer, to which I heard replied more than once, 'No English,' even though they had previously been speaking in broken English.

Usually this would have pissed me off, but in this situation I loved it! They were giving a couple of the border guards fits. It was a thing of beauty. It was a true battle of wits and it was priceless to observe. I wasn't too fond of the border guards at that point, so the fact that the Chinese tourists were pissing them off to such a great extent brought a little joy to my misery.

When the border guard returned he called me back over to the wicket. He had a smile on his face and appeared to be in a much more jovial mood than when I had previously spoken with him.

He was looking at me with a big grin on his face and then he said, 'So, smut poetry, hey?'

'I see you read the letters,' I said to him, now smiling myself.

'Those are some big-time places you're sending those letters to. Sounds like an interesting book you've written.'

'Aim high, buddy. And it is extremely interesting. You're going to want your own copy when it comes out.'

He started asking me about the book. He seemed to be genuinely interested in it and that amused me. After talking about it for a couple of minutes, he finally got down to business.

'Do you know why you were sent in here?'

'Because the first dude I had the pleasure of dealing with has a strange sense of humour? I was actually told it was a 'random check' by the dude.'

'Well, you were going through the Nexus lane but you're not supposed to use Nexus for business.'

'So the search wasn't so random then? Is that what you're saying?'

'It was because of your use of the Nexus lane for something resembling business dealings.'

'I'm sorry, I was unaware of that regulation, but this isn't really business I'm conducting. I'm not making any money off of what I'm doing today.'

He told me that it was still a business dealing in their eyes and that the next time I crossed the border for that reason, I should use the regular lanes, not the Nexus lanes.

Rules for the sake of rules are my favourite! What a bunch of bullshit. I don't know how that makes any sense but I just went along with it as I had little choice in the matter. I have an easier time of figuring out my wife than these rules.

I was nodding my head in agreement as he spoke because I wanted to get the hell out of there, even though I thought it was a load of crap that he was feeding me. Finally, he said to me that I was going to have to pay ten dollars before I could leave. I didn't know how to respond to that, so I just gave him a blank stare in response. Maybe it wasn't so hard to be a border guard after all? The confused look on my face prompted him to ask me if I understood why I had to pay ten dollars for my visit. I told him that I did not understand. I asked him if this was a shakedown. He laughed and then proceeded to spin me a bunch of convoluted, government double-speak of which I understood none.

Getting straight to the point, I asked him what would happen if I refused to pay. He told me that I would be detained. Great, I thought to myself. So now I'm a hostage. I've been kidnapped by the border guards and am being held for a ten dollar ransom. Perfect! To be honest, I was a little disappointed that ten bucks was all I was worth to them.

Of course, I paid the man. I had little choice, really. I wasn't about to be subjected to detainment over a sum so small. They would probably have ragged had I refused to pay. That was a reasonable theory based on the short tempers these dudes seemed to possess. More than likely, they would have done mean and nasty things to me in the back room in retaliation for my dissidence. I figured that a latex-covered finger searching my rectum for drugs would be a lot more painful than parting with my money. Hell, I had a good feeling that Cletus would take no greater joy in the world that to conduct his cavity searches without the use of hands, and that possibility kept me on the straight and narrow.

After paying, the border guard told me to have a good day. He then handed me back my keys, as well as a piece of paper he had signed his initials to. He told me I would need to show the paper to the guard outside in order to leave the premises. I said thanks – for what, I'm not sure – and I left.

As I walked outside, I was stunned by what had just occurred. 'They just shook me down!' I said to myself, aloud. And they had, there was no other way to look at it. I had no idea that the American government was so hard up for money that they had taken to shaking down Canadians coming into their country. I mean, if that had happened to me while crossing the border into Mexico it wouldn't have really surprised me so much. But I was shocked that the United States border guards had taken me for a ride like that. Live and learn.

As I walked back to my truck, Jim-Bob was standing by, a serious frown still on his face. What an idiot he was. I got into the truck and inspected my envelopes to make sure that everything was intact and that the correct envelope was still filled with the corresponding letter. I could tell that they had been rifled through, but everything seemed to be in order. For that small miracle, I was pleased. I still cursed them under my breath for wasting my time and my money.

I fired up my truck, backed out of the spot and then pulled forward, right up to Jim-Bob who was blocking my exit. He told me that I needed to give him the piece of paper the guy inside had given me. I did as I was told.

It was nothing but a little slip of paper with a signature on it, but the hillbilly examined it thoroughly for a good minute in silence, flipping it front to back and back to front, upside down and downside up, over and over again. He appeared to be extremely focused on the piece of paper the entire time. It was as if I had handed him a very complex puzzle and had asked him to solve it. They don't come much dumber than Jim-Bob. I was so glad that he was trusted with carrying a firearm. That really made me feel safe and protected.

Now at that point, I knew that the douchebag was just fucking with me for no other reason than because he could, because that's clearly how he got his kicks in life. But what was I going to do about it? I mean, he had a gun and I'm sure he was just itching for even the slightest of provocations to use it. I really didn't want to be another statistic. Examine away, Billy-Bob. Crack that code.

After thoroughly checking every square millimeter of that little piece of paper, the obese genetic mishap unclipped the radio from his person and called inside. He waited half a minute or so but no one answered. He called again and I heard him say to whoever answered that there was no signature on my paper and he needed to know whether I was allowed to leave or not.

As I could hear what he was saying, I told him, from my truck seat, that there was a signature on the paper, but the bastard completely ignored me. Apparently he couldn't hear me, even though he was standing a mere five feet from my open window.

Eventually, the guy inside that I had been dealing with earlier got on the radio and informed the douchebag that I, indeed, was free to go. The inbred hillbilly, after some deep thought and consideration, stepped out of my way and permitted me to exit, although he took his sweet time about it. I fought the strong urge to run the bastard over as I left. It's been a pleasure, guys. Next time I'll bring lube.

Welcome Home

ABOUT AN HOUR or so after being shaken down by a few of the special folks at United States Border Services, all for the hefty sum of ten dollars, I was on my way back home. I had picked up my books and mailed them out, filled my truck with gas and was now back in line on the Canadian side of things. The line-ups always seem to be much shorter going into Canada than they are going into the USA. I don't know why that is, but it just always seems to be the case. Perhaps harassing decent people and searching Canadian vehicles for absolutely no reason causes delays? It's a theory.

As I inched closer to the border guard booth or kiosk or whatever they call it, I could see that I was in a line that had a woman guard. I immediately let fly a few curses. Now, I love women, much more so than I do men. But here's the thing, I never look forward to dealing with women in any position of authority when that position is one that has traditionally been a man's role, such as a police officer or in this case, a border guard.

More often than not, women are much worse to deal with than their male counterparts. Many of the women in these roles have massive chips on their shoulders. They think they have something to prove and they act accordingly. These power-tripping broads always have to one-up the dudes they work with. If one of her colleagues is a massive asshole, then she'll be a monster asshole just to prove her worth. She'll kick it up a notch higher than the men to prove that she is, indeed, worthy of the job. While her most aggressive colleague may like to operate at a ten, she'll crank it up to eleven. I mean, these chicks have to make up for the lack of a penis somehow. And that, my friends, is why women in roles such as this can often be the biggest bitches on the planet. Needless to say, I was not looking forward to my encounter.

My turn had come and as I approached, I could see that my female border guard meant business. I hadn't spoken to her yet, hadn't even had the chance to piss her off, but she already had a scowl on her face that would have frightened Mike Tyson in his drug-induced, fighting prime. I thought about telling her that she would be a whole lot prettier if she smiled once in a while. I refrained.

Border guard: 'Passport.'

Me: 'Here you go.'

'How long were you gone?'

'An hour, maybe.'

'What were you doing in the USA?'

'I mailed out some books at the Post Office and filled up on gas.'

'Are you bringing anything back with you into Canada?'

'A few review copies of my book. They're going to be mailed out as well.'

'What's the value of the merchandise?'

'You want to know how much my books are worth?'

'Yes, what is the value?'

'They're priceless.'

If she didn't hate me before, she sure did now. She looked angrier than ever, but I had a grin on my face. Loosen up, lady. If you pucker up any tighter you're going to tear a sphincter. Some people are just allergic to laughter. At least I amuse myself.

Her: 'How much did you pay for the books?'

Me: 'Nothing.'

'Sir, how much did the books cost you?'

'They cost me nothing. My publisher had them mailed here – or to Blaine. He paid the printing costs. I'm just picking them up and mailing them out for review because he is overseas right now and time is pressing.'

'Okay sir, I need to know how much you are selling the books for.'

'I'm not selling the books. I already told you, they are going to be mailed out to newspapers and such to be reviewed. I'm not making any money off of them.'

'What is the cover price of the book?'

'I don't think you understand me here. These are my books. I did not buy them and I will not be selling them. I will be giving them away to book reviewers. No profits will be made off of these particular books. Therefore, the government will not be out any revenue if that's what it is that you're worried about.'

There were a few moments of silence that followed. I could see that the wheels were spinning in her head as she was trying to think of what to say to me next. I was enjoying the fact that I was pissing her off while, at the same time, doing absolutely nothing wrong. After a few more moments, she had finally decided upon her next move.

'Let me see one of the books.'

'Here you go.'

She took the book in hand and began to examine it. When she saw the cover picture, which was the statue of David (the latest edition has a scantily clad woman on the cover because my publisher is a pig) and then read the title which is *Let Me Put My Poems in You*, I could tell that she was caught off-guard. I could see that she wanted to laugh, but she covered it up well. She had a good poker face.

'This is your book, sir?'

'It sure is. Check out the picture on the back cover. That handsome man strongly resembles this guy right here, doesn't he?'

She flipped to the back cover and stared at the picture for a few moments before thumbing quickly through the book. She then returned it to me and informed me that the retail value of the book was written on the back cover and that I was going to have to go inside and pay duty on the value of the books. As you can imagine, I was not pleased. Although, I was relatively certain that she was just looking for an excuse to give me a strip search.

At that point I'd had enough of her bullshit and was tired of being falsely treated like a criminal all day long, by both Americans and Canadians. But instead of getting angry, I turned up the charm.

I informed her, in a slightly flirtatious tone (no lady is immune), that there were only 18 books in the truck, and again I let her know that they were all going out to reviewers, free of charge, and that therefore

I would be making no money at all off of them. Therefore, the government would not be out any potential revenue. I told her that it was such an odd number of books to have because I had just mailed out the rest of them to be reviewed in the United States and overseas, also not for profit.

This woman, I am sure, was not used to a man being so nice and mildly flirtatious with her. She wasn't bad-looking at all, but the scowl on her face and her bitchy personality would put the vast majority of dudes off, for sure.

She finally came around to seeing my point of view and decided to let me through. She only did so after warning me that if I did the same deed again, she would take me inside and charge me duty (what the hell is *duty* anyway?). I told her, through a smile, that this was the first and last time I would be bringing books across the border. She then handed me back my passport and told me that I could be on my way. I told her to enjoy the rest of her day and was gone. She wanted me.

I hate crossing the border and that day was a strong example of why. I was held up for an extended period of time, interrogated and shaken down for money by representatives of the United States government. Then I was interrogated again by my own border agency and was almost forced to pay duty on my books in order to get back into my own country. I was treated without much respect or kindness by most of the guards I dealt with, while a couple of them obviously went out of their way to be huge assholes. Clearly border guards are some of the biggest douchebags going.

Because of these incidents, and another incident that followed about two weeks later (a story for another time), I now carry a bottle of lubricant in my glove compartment. It's just a matter of time until I get the rubber glove treatment and if I do, I'm at least going to squeeze half that bottle of lube out onto the searching finger before it goes a routing.

This is a message for all you border guards out there, or at least those of you who are literate: if you want to get your profession off of my douchebag list of professions, stop giving me such a hard time whenever I cross the border. I am not smuggling drugs, weapons or children. I do not have over ten grand in cash on me and I do not have hidden compartments all over my vehicle, filled to the brim with guns and drugs. I also do not have baggies of cocaine inserted up my rectum. All I want is to cross the border in peace, that's it.

If you are a border guard, study my face on the cover of this book and commit it to memory. Then make everyone you work with buy a copy of my book and tell them to study my face as well so that the next time I cross the border, you will all know who I am and instead of wanting to interrogate and strip search me, you will simply ask me to autograph your books. On the other hand, if you are a young and sexy female border guard (also known as a unicorn – but I'm sure you do exist somewhere), the next time I cross the border please, take me to your secluded room and strip-search the hell out of me and I'll still autograph your book. And just because I am a gentleman, I'll also strip search you right back. You can never be too safe. I've got to look out for number one. Maybe you've keistered a weapon or something. It would be irresponsible of me to not check.

CHAPTER 14

URINAL ETIQUETTE

IF YOU'RE a lady reader, you might be wondering why I'm writing a chapter about urinal etiquette. You're probably thinking that few things in life should be easier for a man than to stand and pee. I mean, you're most likely thinking that a man just needs to point and shoot. How difficult can that be?

In general, the principle behind urinal usage is rudimentary. It can be summed up as such: piss in the urinal. That sounds pretty simple, right? I think so. I have personally never had a problem with it. I would assume that most boys from about the age of three onward have a pretty firm grasp of it. However, based on what I see often enough when using public facilities, I appear to be in the minority when it comes to the honed urinal skills I possess.

When I'm out on the town and I need to pee, I treat the porcelain public piss tank just like I would my very own toilet at home - that is, I pee directly into it. But for the apparent hordes of urinal-challenged douchebags out there, pissing into the vessel is simply far too complex a task to handle.

Even when I've been drunk out of my mind at the bar - shitfaced, to the lay person - and have had to use the facilities, I have always managed to piss into the urinal. At least that's my story and I'm sticking to it. I've never voided my entire bladder onto the floor in front of the damn thing. It's a pretty big bowl, usually mounted to the wall at crotch level. For those of us coordinated enough to do such things as unzip our pants, it's a pretty hard target to miss.

But for certain douchebags out there, life apparently isn't worth living if it involves pissing into urinals. It would appear as if it is much more satisfying to cover the entire bathroom floor in urine. They must feel that the rest of us enjoy splashing the soles of our shoes through a stranger's urine pool as we manoeuvre our way to the crowded piss troughs in bars and in stadium facilities at intermission.

This really pisses me off. When I go to take a leak at the pub, I don't want to be forced to stand in a sea of some dumb asshole's urine. If I'm at the game, then odds are the soles of my shoes are already covered in copious amounts of spilled beer, nacho cheese and popcorn, so the last thing I need to add to the concoction is some ignorant douchebag's used beer.

Someday I hope to stumble into a public washroom and witness one of those douchebags in the act of micturating on the floor. Nothing would please me more than to trip him face first onto the tile floor and force him to lick up his own mess. That is unless he happens to be a man the size of Shaq, in which case I would kindly keep all my hostility bottled up inside. I'm not suicidal. As much as it bugs me, it's still only urine. It's not worth losing my life over. I can hold it.

Chin Up, Eyes Forward

THERE ARE MANY unwritten rules in life, and for good reason. An unwritten rule of urinal usage is the 'eyes forward' rule.

No man enjoys standing immediately adjacent to another man while urinating, at least not any man I know. It can be a little awkward at times to stand hip to hip with a stranger while you both have your penises hanging out of your pants.

That awkwardness becomes amplified when pissing beside someone with wandering eyes. Aside from being creepy and just plain wrong, it's a sure way to get yourself a black eye if you let your eyes wander over to another man's penis while he's pissing, so don't do it. Your eyes should want to be anywhere but on the penis of another man. I shouldn't even need to tell you that.

This unwritten rule, however, doesn't seem to be known by some of the weirdoes out there. These socially inappropriate idiots bounce into the bathroom and bound right up to the urinal that's directly beside you, then try to strike up a conversation while looking you straight in the face. Not even your best buddy would act in such a fashion, yet this perfect stranger finds it completely appropriate to stare at you while you both piss side by each, dicks in hands.

These douchebags are far too comfortable in situations where being moderately uncomfortable is normal and being overly comfortable is creepy. A man who is overtly comfortable standing directly beside another man and urinating is a man that I don't want to be standing beside while urinating.

No man enjoys it when an oddly friendly weirdo saddles up to him, too close for comfort, especially so when his penis is out of his pants and in his hand. Even more so when that weirdo is looking all over the place, eyes darting everywhere except for where they should be, which is straight ahead of him.

Conversation between two men standing beside each other at the urinal should fall into the category of slim to none, at least if you are strangers. If I don't know you from Adam, do not come up beside me while I'm pissing and chat me up like a gossip girl, all the while looking me up and down.

One of these days you're going to exude your strange behaviour beside the wrong guy and he's either going to kick your ass or pound it. If you are 'that guy' and you are reading this book right now, take my warning to heart. It just might save your life, or your anus.

Common Sense Is Not So Common

THERE ARE MANY THINGS that happen in the men's washroom that make me shake my head in utter disbelief. The extreme lack of common sense displayed by certain guys can be staggering.

In case one of you morons, to which I am referring, happens to be reading this book, and I hope you are so that you might learn a thing or two, let me lay a few things out for you. First of all, if you walk into a men's room to take a piss and there are more than two urinals hanging on the wall, and there is already one guy in there doing his business, do not choose the urinal directly beside him.

Whenever possible, always leave at least one urinal of space between you and another man. I call it a buffer urinal. If it is possible to leave even more urinals of space in between the two of you, then do so. Unless the man who is already in there is some sort of a freak or a weirdo himself, he's going to think that there is something seriously wrong with you if you have your choice between several urinals yet still select the one directly beside him. Either that or you're going to get yourself a date for next weekend.

Here's another lesson for you creepy douchebags. Once you have finished, a shake of the unit is, of course, necessary. But if you stand there for a full minute, shake it profusely, then slow it down, then pause, then resume furious shaking, you are no longer flopping off the drips but are now masturbating in a public toilet. Being caught pleasuring yourself in the men's room is a sure way to wind up in the emergency room.

Also, do not leave the public restroom without first washing your hands. I don't care if you didn't piss directly onto your hands and I don't care if you don't wash your hands at home. There are still other people in there and they will notice if you just walk straight past them, out of the restroom, without putting so much as a splash of water to your hands. And especially if you've been laying down a number two in the stall, for the love of God wash your damn hands, you filthy bastard! I certainly don't want to grab the door handle after you have palmed it with your pissy and shitty hands. Don't be a douchebag.

CHAPTER 15

JUSTICE IS BLIND... AND RETARDED

OUR JUSTICE SYSTEM is broken. It is in utter disarray. The comings and goings of the judicial process make about as much sense as one of Charlie Sheen's drug-fuelled and incoherent rants (all joking aside, you're still my idol, Charlie). The justice system is a botched abortion of what it should be. It's a disgusting mess. It should be dropped into a giant shredder and then disposed of in a vat of acid.

We should, instead, have a society where vigilante justice is not only practiced but encouraged. Bring Spiderman and Superman out of retirement. Honestly, where have those guys been anyway?

A vigilante world is the kind of world I would like to live in. You steal from me, I break your leg... and justice is served. Get rid of judges and lawyers. They're the root of the problem anyway. Sack-less douchebag judges and morally stunted lawyers perpetuate the revolving door of justice. They should all be rounded up and shipped off to Antarctica where they can be left to fend for themselves. I doubt they'd be missed.

Take Me Drunk, I'm Home

WHY IS IT THAT in this wonderful country of ours, most crimes are apparently okay to commit as long as the perpetrator was drunk when the crime was carried out? It seems, to me, that drunkenness is the ultimate defence to any crime.

'Oh, you were drunk when you killed your husband. That means you weren't really thinking clearly, were you? I'm sure spending five years in prison will more than suffice for your drunken crime of passion. I'm sure it will satisfy your dead husband's grieving friends and family to know that you will serve five years in prison for taking his life in cold blood in hopes of cashing in on his life insurance policy. I'm sure they will find that sentence more than satisfactory for the crime committed.' – Something that has probably been said by a douchebag judge several times throughout his useless career.

If I've learned anything from watching the news, it's that if I ever plan on committing a crime, I most certainly will get drunk before I do it, or at the very least in the immediate aftermath. The vast majority of sentences appear to be substantially reduced in duration if the perpetrator happened to be drunk at the time of the offence.

The exception is driving offenses. You can pretty much get away with any driving offense, as long as you're not found to have been under the influence of drugs or alcohol. Doesn't matter how blatant a disregard you show towards people's lives, it would appear as if no crime committed by a sober mind while behind the wheel can be punishable by law.

A few years back, just a few minutes by car south of where I live, a man was driving home one night with his kids in the back seat of his vehicle. He was drunk. He was on the highway and decided to change lanes. He did so without signalling or shoulder checking and he ran the side of his vehicle directly into a motorcycle rider, sending the rider violently off of his bike, crashing to the pavement. Oh, and by the way, the driver of the vehicle, the drunk who was driving with his kids in the back seat of the car, happened to be a local, off-duty police officer. What an outstanding citizen!

After the collision, the police officer, who had been trained in CPR, did not pull over and stop to see if he could help the motorcycle rider that he had so brutally removed from his bike. He, instead, fled the scene and took his kids home, leaving the motorcyclist alone to die.

Returning to the scene of the crime some time later, without his children, the perpetrator was breathalysed, found to be drunk, and taken into custody. The douchebag had claimed that he had not been driving drunk at the time of the accident. He stated that he had fled the scene merely to take his children home so that they would not have to witness what had happened to the man on the bike and be traumatized by it. He also claimed that he had not been driving drunk at the time of the accident, but that he had taken a couple drinks once he had arrived home with his children in order to calm his shattered nerves. That poor man. It must be really stressful making pancakes out of motorcyclists. We should all shed a tear for the wonderful man.

Time passed and the officer was suspended from duty, with full pay of course, while an investigation took place. Eventually all the charges were dropped and the police officer was reinstated to his job.

This is a situation where sentencing would have been more severe if the douchebag were found to have been drunk during the accident. But the rectal discharge in a judge's robe believed the cop when he said that he was not drunk at the time of the crash, and only had half a bottle of vodka afterwards to calm his delicate nerves.

According to our courts, crashing into someone with your vehicle while driving sober does not warrant the same consequences as hitting someone while drunk. It is, perhaps, the only situation where being drunk would most likely result in harsher punishment. This cop was drunk while driving, so he should have received a harsh punishment, but he knew the perfect defence. Case closed. Good for him.

This incident is more shocking because it involves a cop. I'm not writing this to try to make cops look like assholes (although there are enough of them out there), it's just that this story has more shock value because the public holds police officers to a higher standard than the general public − or at least in some neighbourhoods they do. I mean, this man is supposed to be out protecting and serving the public, not recklessly endangering and killing. This douchebag deserved to have the book thrown at him hard. He should have been locked up, he should have lost his job, and child services should have stepped in to protect his children from their drunk-driving, murderous father. But instead he was let free to roam the streets, still in uniform, and to live to kill another day. The justice system clearly has the victim's rights at the forefront, doesn't it?

If you kill someone while driving drunk (unless you are a cop) you will go to prison. However, if you kill someone while driving sober, most likely you will do no time behind bars. That doesn't sit right with me.

If anything, you have an excuse to make mistakes when you are drunk. The excuse is that you are drunk. 'Why are there muddy footprints all over the floor, honey?' Sorry, I was drunk last night when I came home. 'Why didn't you lift the toilet seat before taking a piss, my dear?' Oh, sorry babe, I was drunk and it was dark. 'Who's that naked girl curled up asleep on the shag rug by the fire?' I'm not sure. Holy shit was I ever wasted last night! So was she, apparently. I'll go find her clothes.

While inebriation can be amusing and a wonderful excuse for certain behaviours, if you kill someone, you should be proven at fault and you should go to prison. You should also be found at fault and go to prison if you are sober.

If you change lanes into a motorbike and kill a rider while you are driving sober, you have no excuse whatsoever for your careless behaviour. You clearly have no respect for the lives of anyone around you and should therefore serve time for your careless actions. Driving is not a right, it's a privilege (or so I've heard), and one that you no longer deserve to have if you recklessly kill people while exercising your privilege.

To make a long story short, don't be a douchebag behind the wheel! The two thousand pounds of steel you're piloting can kill people, so pay attention and show respect to others. Don't let me catch you being a douchebag out there. I will run you off the road and bitch-slap you, vigilante style.

Life? Whose Life?

WHY IS IT THAT someone can be sentenced to life in prison, only to be released the following decade, or even sooner, as long as they are sentenced in Canada? Is it because the judge didn't specify whose lifespan the sentence was based on? Is it the life of a kid with cystic fibrosis? Is it the life of a Chihuahua? I'm sorry, but to me a life sentence should mean that you are in prison for the rest of your own life. It's that simple. The math is sound. If you are a severely violent, repulsive and dangerous human being who prolifically rapes and murders, I'm sure most people would feel much safer were you to be locked away for the duration of your actual life.

I had a law teacher in high school who was a pretty funny guy. He had a dry sense of humour, so a lot of the slower kids didn't get him. A teacher that's not afraid to speak his mind or to be politically incorrect is a breath of fresh air in a constipated education system.

This teacher used to always tell us, jokingly… I assumed, that if we ever planned on committing a crime, that we should first get drunk. Then he would joke about how one woman could single-handedly kill several of her own husbands throughout her lifetime if she were drunk every time she committed an act of murder.

My teacher explained that with early parole from a 'life sentence,' the husband-killing wife could be out of prison as early as seven years after killing her husband. She could then remarry, kill again (while drunk, of course), spend another seven years of a 'life sentence' in prison, only to be released one more time. It was an ongoing joke he would make, but the sad truth about it is that it was based on a seriously ridiculous reality.

All these pathetic judges that allow severe injustices to happen should be sentenced to life in prison themselves. For all the harm they have thrust upon society by allowing repeat offenders to continually be freed from prison to commit more crimes, they should rot themselves.

How many rapes and murders, bank robberies and convenience store candy bar thefts are judges personally responsible for? I'm willing to bet a lot: probably even more than a dozen. They let dangerous nut jobs and sugar junkie kleptomaniacs off the hook, time and time again, most likely because of some obscure precedence, government mandate or the fact that releasing the bad guys back into the wild is good for job security. They also let horrible dudes out of prison far too early just because the inmate had a clever lawyer with a gift for double-speak or because the prisoner showed outstanding behaviour while behind bars by not killing or raping other inmates. Good for him, by the way. If you are a judge, give yourself a reality check, and maybe a punch to the scrotum, if you have one. Stop being such a habitual douchebag and actually do your job properly, for the love of God, and keep the streets safe for the rest of us. And don't forget the children. Think about the children!

CHAPTER 16

SHOW ME THE MONEY

THE PURSUIT of the almighty dollar is the driving force behind many a bad behaviour. There's a reason why they say that money is the root of all evil (who is the 'they' that we always reference?). Whether you're a billionaire CEO, some bum on the street or a stripper working the pole, life's all about making that next dollar.

And who can blame anyone for the pursuit of the dollar? I hope that I sell a million copies of this book and headline a world-wide comedy tour so that I can afford that Ferrari I've always wanted, not to mention a house on the beach to go with it. So, I also like money and want more of it, but what I have no tolerance for are human beings who will stop at nothing in order to make their money. I can't stand those money-hungry assholes. They're destroying society. To steal a word from the lexicon of literary genius George W. Bush, those bastards are evildoers.

Those who cause undo harm to people, animals or the environment, just to maximize profits, should be euthanized. You know who I'm talking about.

No Profit Is Profit Enough

MANY LARGE COMPANIES and corporations have been working hard for years, attempting to turn First World countries into Third World ones, just to maximize their profits. The sad part is that they are achieving their goals, and we are sitting idly by allowing it to happen.

We are all aware of these big-box and multibillion-dollar companies that turn disgustingly high profits while paying the vast majority of their employees next to nothing. Wealthy companies that pay a large percentage of their employees less than living wages all while they turn multimillion or multibillion dollar profits are disgusting businesses run by morally reprehensible douchebags. I wish they could be stopped.

Call me old fashioned, but I believe that if a company turns a great profit, their employees should be rewarded in turn. It only makes sense to compensate the people responsible for the good and hard work that has helped the company get to such heights. This may sound too simple, but if people are well paid, they will inherently have more money to spend. If they have money to spend, they will pump it back into the economy, which will benefit businesses such as the ones they work for. To the ultra-right wing, that probably sounds like communist speak, but they are horrible fascists, so fuck 'em.

The owners and operators of these big, douchebag-run companies don't really give a shit about human beings though. The big wigs make big profits for themselves and the rest of the fat bastards at the top of the heap, and therefore could not care less about the people at the bottom, many of whom live at or near poverty level.

The practices of big-time businessmen and stock market hustlers, practices that are allowed to occur, in part, because of the self-indulgent influence of extremely right-wing politicians, are essentially responsible for ruining the economy. They have done so by paying people increasingly lower and unliveable wages while exponentially increasing their own salaries and profits. The middle class is being wiped out in North America and Europe. Sadly, a society without a middle class is indicative of a Third World country. I'm pissed because I don't want to live in a Third World country, dammit!

This type of disgusting shit happens all the time. A large company has a fantastic year, achieving record-breaking profits. But instead of giving everyone a pat on the back and a bonus check, the company proceeds to downsize frontline staff levels, cutback the wages of everyone not in upper-management, and close plants in the west and move them to somewhere in southeast Asia.

Basically, once the greedy few at the top get a taste of a large sum of money, the only way to get that high feeling again is to make even more money the following year. What's more fun than buying a brand new Ferrari? Buying a brand new Ferrari every year, that's what. It's a vicious cycle of extreme greed and it is ruining the world. I sound like my mother.

Greed is like a disease, a disease that is spreading furiously fast. Greed has always existed and it has always been at the root of many an evil. The only difference, as far as I'm concerned, between greed of the past and greed of the present is that greed was once something to be frowned upon.

Throughout time, greed has been treated by society as something that was unacceptable and wrong. Most people were taught by their parents and peers that it was much better to be generous and fair than to hoard. These days, however, greed has not only become acceptable but is strongly encouraged.

The greedy douchebags at the top have become idolized by the masses. Their excessive greed has become a trait that people admire instead of despise. It has created a shift in the public's moral values, and much of the masses are too stupid to realize the harm in it.

Like I've said before, I have no problem with money. I'd love to have a ton of it. But while I like money, I don't *love* money. No one should *love* money. We are sometimes willing to do unspeakable things for that which we love. Money should not be one of those things. Work hard for it, strive to earn more of it, but don't kill, wound and impoverish the masses in order to increase your wealth.

Screw The Environment, I Need a Bigger Yacht

IF AN ENVIRONMENTAL law or regulation is in the way of making you bigger profits than what you currently make, there's no need to worry. All you have to do is buy yourself a politician or two. Oil and gas companies do it all the time. Having a politician – or even better, an entire political party - in your back pocket can really open up some big doors.

Would it save your natural gas company a lot of time and money if you could just dispose your toxic chemical waste products by dumping them into marshlands or into rivers and farmlands? Oh hell ya it would! No longer having to pay for proper clean-ups and disposals of large quantities of hazardous chemicals would certainly increase your profit margins. If you could bypass those pesky, senseless regulations, your company would no longer be turning great profits, it would be turning amazing profits. Yippee cay yeah!

So what if you poison the drinking water of all the people and animals around your drilling sites? So what if you cause strange sicknesses and rare cancers to spread throughout the people and animals that live in the areas surrounding your plants and work sites? Who cares if farmlands are destroyed and there aren't any potato crops next year? You – the big cheese at the top collecting those massive checks - don't personally live in that area, and you think that all the people who live in those areas are just stupid hillbillies anyway. All that matters is that you can make yourself even richer by not having to worry about following proper practices and clean-up procedures. Clearly, dollars are all that really matter to you. So what if a few hundred or thousand people have to suffer and die along the path to your own personal wealth and success? Screw them for being in the way.

Some may think that this unethical behaviour would be hard to perpetrate because of the governmental regulations that are in place to protect people and the environment. Those people would be mistaken. Side-stepping environmental safety regulations is something that is really not at all that difficult. All you have to do is make a powerful politician one of your 'business partners' or drop some money in his, or his party's, coffers and watch as regulations and obstacles magically disappear before your very eyes, allowing you to get away with any number of unethical and illegal behaviours. I sure hope that all those greedy sociopaths can take all their money to hell with them. If not, they're going to be pissed!

Even if a company happens to get caught breaking the law by illegally dumping toxic waste, it's not usually a big deal. The associated penalties are often so meagre that it is much more affordable to pay the fines for illegal dumping than it is to dispose of the waste in a proper and ethical fashion.

Sometimes fines for the illegal dumping of toxic waste can be as little as five or ten thousand dollars. On the flip side, disposing of the waste in a safe and proper manner could cost dozens of times more than the fines. If you remove all your ethics, morals and scruples from the equation, it's a very easy decision to make.

I was watching *The Colbert Report* in the wake of the Gulf oil disaster and they had a bit on their show that was along the lines of what I'm talking about. Stephen Colbert was talking about Dawn (the soap company) and how they were putting commercials on television illustrating that their soap could help remove oil from oil-soaked wildlife. They were trying to encourage the public to buy their soap by saying that the company would donate a dollar from every bottle sold to the oil spill disaster. The irony of the situation is that Dawn soap is made from oil.

Colbert then made the 'accusation' that the Dawn soap company, in an attempt to maximize profits, was responsible for the Gulf oil disaster. By spilling oil, their oil-based product was used and sold as a remedy to some of the disaster spill's problems.

Here's a little tidbit for you: A man named Richard J. Ferris was on the Board of Directors of British Petroleum (BP). In case you didn't know, BP was responsible for the gulf oil spill. Ferris was also a 'non-executive director' of Procter and Gamble (P&G), the company that makes Dawn.

It's sure hard to put a funny spin on this bullshit. I sure hope you are learning, though. If I can't make you laugh, the least I can do is educate. I just wanted to make you all question where it is that you get your products and energy from.

Natural gas, for example, may just be ruining the environment around you without you even realizing it. Sure, it's clean-burning, and the word 'natural' is right there in the title, but the most common process of obtaining it from the rock beneath you is anything but clean, safe and natural. And the reason you don't realize it is because you don't see these stories on the news very often. And why is that the case? Well, guess who owns the news companies? I'm coming off like a crazy, conspiracy theorist, aren't I? I lay the blame on the near empty bottle of whisky on my nightstand.

CHAPTER 17

THE CORPORATE GIANT

IT'S JUST A SIGN of the times. Mum and Pop stores are a thing of the past. Small companies are almost no longer. That family-run corner store at the end of the block just closed down. Hank's Hardware store was bought out, shut down and subsequently replaced by some massive store with the word 'depot' or 'warehouse' in the name.

Big box stores and the multi-national, multibillion-dollar corporations run it all these days. There's one big man on campus that has either bought out or destroyed all others in sight so that he can reign supreme. He's rich as fuck, and probably dickhead.

He has forced the little guy right out of the market by making his company impossible to compete with. He deals in much larger volumes than his competitors and, therefore, he can undersell the competition and run them into the ground. He also pays much lower salaries than his competitors, another fantastic way to keep costs down and profits up. He is a corporate douchebag, but he rules the world and there's nothing you can do about it.

If greed were a human being, he would be king of the world right now. I feel quite safe in saying that our planet has never before seen the extreme level of greed that is now exhibited daily by the world's elite. No sum is ever enough, especially not for giant corporations. No matter the cost and harm to the insignificant people beneath them, profits have to be maximized and expenses downsized. The rich must get richer and they do so at the expense of everyone and everything else, no matter the collateral damage. There was a recent report that stated the wealthiest thirty six people in the world collectively have more money than the poorest three and a half billion people on the planet, which is roughly half the planet's population. That doesn't make you feel good, does it? Thirty six people have more money than fifty percent of the world. And I guarantee you they aren't satisfied with percentage and won't be pleased until they have more collective wealth than the remainder of the world combined.

Mo' Money

IN ORDER TO MAXIMIZE profits for the few at the top of the food chain, corporations are famous for cutbacks. I realize that when times are tough, certain things have to be cut and downsized. I mean, if you just got laid-off from work, you may need to cancel your subscription to HBO. If you can't afford to eat, maybe paying for premium cable isn't the best move at the moment. The problem is that many of these big companies cutback in all the wrong places and cutback when it is completely unnecessary.

It is despicable, but common, practice that the top dogs of these companies make more money when times are tough because they get bonuses for cutting back production workers' wages, benefits and jobs. They often overlook the real problems and ignore the easiest and biggest adjustments they could make, such as trimming the fat at the top, because that would take money away from people that desperately can't do without Bentleys and personal chauffeurs. Rewarding those who do the least with bonuses for cutting back the number of employees who do the most is an unethical, questionable yet unfortunately common business practice.

Ruining people's lives just so that you can afford yet another exotic vacation home is reprehensible. But then I'm not a sociopathic asshole absent of a conscience, so how would I understand?

Rich douchebags are trying to turn Canada, the USA and much of Europe into Third World countries by attempting to eliminate the middle class. Middle class jobs are disappearing by the bucket load for no other reason than to make the already wealthy even wealthier.

It's not just in the private sector that this bullshit behavior occurs. It is often in the public sector as well. In a hospital, for instance, where a janitor used to get paid a decent living wage, the cleaning services have now been contracted out to the lowest tender. The once decently paid janitor is then let go and offered back his job by the new contractor, but at half his original wage and without a pension plan this time around. Take it or leave it.

As a result, the hospital now saves a great deal of money. And for being the man to pull the trigger on the operation, the douchebag senior manager at the top gets a nice bonus cheque. That useless idiot gets to keep a small percentage of the money he saved the hospital, just for himself. I hope his wife divorces him one day for a young, sexy janitor and takes all his precious money with her.

How are you supposed to survive or support a family if your already modest salary is suddenly cut in half? How can the economy sustain itself if the majority of people contributing to the economy are getting poorer by the year, inherently spending less cash, all while inflation is perpetually on the rise?

The cream of the crop running many government and private industries simply aren't concerned with those kinds of questions. The scum at the top get to suck all they want from the company tit. They are financially comfortable and that is all that matters to them. Screw everyone else. Maybe the peasants will get tossed a bone, from time to time, and they will like it.

For many of these fat cats, I believe they eventually get to a point where there is no longer any trace of humanity left in them. They no longer see people as human beings – they can only see people as cockroaches.

I hope these greedy sociopaths one day lose all their money in the bipolar stock market and are forced to feel the same financial pain that they have inflicted on so many others over the years. Or that the next Bernie Madoff takes them, and all their money, for a wonderful ride. They deserve nothing less than to feel the same pain they have needlessly inflicted on others.

Helping Others?

MANY YEARS AGO, shortly after automobile production began in the United States, Henry Ford was struggling to sell cars. He wanted to dramatically increase sales of his automobiles and he had a revolutionary idea to enable him to do so.

Like a mad man – or a deranged lunatic, if you will – he decided that he would start paying his employees good wages. The crazy bastard thought that if he were to increase all his employees' wages that they would in turn have more disposable income and would, as a result, be able to afford to buy his cars.

So he implemented his absurd idea and, the crazy thing is that it worked. The decision was good for jobs, good for job security, good for business and good for society and the economy.

His employees were able to properly support their families and, more importantly to Mr. Ford, they were able to buy his cars. His employees were happier, cared more about their jobs, and worked harder because they felt as if they were valued.

So, Henry Ford actually increased his profits by – get this – paying his employees more money. What a crazy concept to grasp.

It didn't take much time for other businesses to follow suit. Before long, people everywhere were making good money and businesses were thriving because people had money to spend. The economy was doing well, people were doing well. It was win–win. It was complete and total madness!

Of course, the world is a different place now than it was back in Henry Ford's day, but I believe the general concept would still hold true. If everyone earned better wages, there would be more money to go around. More money would be spent and put back into the economy, thus creating larger demands for goods and services, thus creating more jobs and creating larger profits for companies.

But today we have the opposite practice of what Henry Ford did to maximize sales and profit. We have stores such as Wal-Mart and Target that pay their employees next to nothing. Therefore, their employees can't afford to shop anywhere else.

Because Wal-Mart's products are all made in places like China, where the cost of human labour is exponentially cheaper than in North America, they can buy and sell their products for less than their competition, further chasing companies and the good jobs that come with them away from North America. What ever happened to trade tariffs to protect the local economy?

Perhaps companies like Wal-Mart are more similar to Henry Ford than I thought. While his product was expensive, requiring people to have lots of money in order to purchase the cars, Wal-Mart and their fellow company's products are inexpensive. Therefore, if these companies paid their employees higher wages, they would be able to shop at better stores and buy themselves better things than Wal-Mart has to offer.

This would mean that less people would shop at Wal-Mart and therefore their profits would decrease. So maybe they are not paying employees low wages to maximize profits in the obvious way, they are paying them low wages so that they have no choice but to shop at Wal-Mart. They cannot afford to shop anywhere else.

I feel like I just solved a mystery or discovered something that was not supposed to be discovered. My heart's racing right now and I'm starting to get a little nervous, although maybe that's just because I've been up far too long writing and drinking scotch.

If I suddenly go 'missing' once this book is published (and that crazy bastard Cheney's not to blame), you will all know that one of these companies' henchmen have got me and that I have been murdered or deported to Siberia.

You conspiracy theorists reading this should take this info and run with it. I hope I'm not getting really carried away over nothing. I have had a lot of scotch to drink tonight and therefore may have built this up in my head to be much more than it actually is. Anyway, if I am murdered, this book will probably sell millions of copies in stores like Wal-Mart and I will become posthumously rich and famous. I really hope that they make a 'Matthew James Day' somewhere to remember my awesomeness. Promise me that.

CHAPTER 18

DRESSED FOR NO SUCCESS

DOUCHEBAGS CAN POP up out of nowhere at work or at the pub. You may see them at the gym or they may be on your hockey team. They can sneak up on you anywhere and everywhere.

There are certain people who are such obvious douchebags that they couldn't sneak up on you even if you were blindfolded and semi-concussed in the eye of a hurricane. These losers are about as subtle as a grenade. Everything about these idiots oozes and drips douchebag, from their ridiculous haircuts and hats right down to their comical shoes.

The way you look and dress says a lot about who you are. They say clothes make the man (again, who are *they*?), and many a douchebag chooses clothing that fits exactly who he is at heart.

We've all seen them. Sometimes you can't even hold back your laughter as they pass by. They're those fools whose creepy appearances bring vomit to the mouths of women and disgust to the faces of real men everywhere.

Dude Looks Like a Lady

I DON'T CARE for the term 'manscaping.' It's just a word that some men use to try to make the girly things that they do to themselves sound less feminine. They blend two manly words together, 'man' and 'landscaping,' into an oh-so-clever term that basically means you shape your eyebrows, wax your chest, and get facials and pedicures.

Just because you squish two manly words into one, it doesn't make the womanly behaviour you describe with the word any less feminine. Manscaping isn't fooling anybody, tough guy. There's no way to man-up your leg waxing and spa treatments, so stop trying.

Real men are hairy. We can have bushy eyebrows, hairy chests and legs, and even hairy backs (sorry ladies, we don't like that anymore than you do). Hairy is just how God made us. We don't look like women and that's because we are not women. And, if I'm not mistaken, that's what makes most women attracted to us: the fact that we are men.

Have you ever found yourself out in public, just staring at some random guy's face trying to figure out what the hell was wrong with him? Then, coming to the realisation that he's bucked down and removed half of his eyebrows and sculpted them into an unnatural shape, you finally discover what's making him look like a full-grown weirdo. I'm sure most of you know what I'm talking about (or maybe you don't, what do I know?). Why in the hell would you want to look like such a fool? Is it an unwritten rule of the douchebag code that you've got to make yourself look as creepy as possible? It probably is, actually.

Now, I'm not saying that a man can't clean up an unruly hair or two, here and there, or even shave his back to impress the ladies by looking a little more man-like and a little less ape-like. And I understand that if you have a unibrow you may want to pull a couple hairs out in order to make your lone eyebrow into two distinct eyebrows. That's only natural. But completely changing the shape of your eyebrows, unless you are a woman, makes you look creepy and weird, two key characteristics of the douchebag.

It is also not uncommon for a douchebag to exhibit other lady traits, such as carrying a purse and wearing earrings. I mean, there's the odd guy out there that can pull off looking cool with earrings, but those guys are few and far between, and most of them are rockstars (in case you were wondering, rockstars fall under an entirely different set of rules from the average man, and no, I don't know why, it's just a law of nature).

For the most part, a guy with an earring looks like a complete douchebag. Especially when the earring clad man is old, gray-haired and balding. Then he really looks like an over-the-hill creep trying unsuccessfully to hang onto his youth. Go out gracefully, Grandpa!

Sometimes I feel like I've slipped into the twilight zone and I'm the only real man left on this planet. When a dude bumps into me with his man-purse slung over his shoulder and then looks at me with a bitchy expression on his un-masculine face, as if I'm an inconvenience because I'm standing in the way of him and his enormous purse, a bigger douchebag I could not have encountered. Unless you awoke to find your tool box broken and you were forced, in a quick pinch, to take your wife's purse to work for the day to carry your tools, there is no valid excuse for a man to carry a purse of his own. None. Not ever.

Pretty Fly For a White Guy

THERE IS ONE LOOK, above all others, that screams douchebag. If you carry this look, you might as well hike to the highest mountaintop with a megaphone to yell for the whole world to hear that you are an enormous douchebag.

Let's start at the top and work our way down for this ultimate douchebag look because there is just so much to cover. First of all, you wear a hat, most likely a baseball cap, and escaping from all sides may well be your greasy, unwashed hair.

Your hat has a completely straight brim, of course, not even a slight bend is visible, the universal douchebag sign. You also do not wear your hat with the brim coming straight forward off your forehead, how it's meant to be worn, or even straight backwards. You wear it at all sorts of strange angles, pretty much any angle between straight forward and straight backward, which are, in case you were unaware, the only two acceptable angles for a hat to be worn at.

Underneath your hat, there may very well be a bandana. In order for you to showcase the oh-so awesome and tough-looking bandana, you don't pull your hat down all the way. Instead, your hat sits quite high up on top of your head, making you look like even more of a fool.

You wear very large, excessively ugly sunglasses at all times. Whether you're outside or inside, day or night, you've got your goofy-assed glasses on your face. Maybe it's because you think they're night vision goggles and that they improve your eyesight in the darkness? Maybe it's because you're dumber than a tea party affiliate and you actually think it is cool to wear your shades indoors and at night. Either way, you need to ditch the shades, cool guy. Then go out and buy yourself a manly pair – ones that don't have rhinestones encrusted on them - and only wear them when there is actually sun in the sky and your eyes need protection. I know that sounds crazy, but that's why sunglasses were invented.

Around your neck is a large gold chain, quite possibly with a massive cross hanging from it. Even though you are not Catholic, you wear the cross because you think it makes you look bad-ass, because that's the look Jesus was going for when he was hanging from the cross.

You wear a skin tight, sleeveless, ribbed undershirt at all times (aka, a wife-beater). Sometimes you wear it as a shirt all on its own, other times you wear it underneath a buttoned up shirt that is never actually buttoned up when you wear it. Now, some real men wear undershirts for doing manual labour such as yard work, but you douchebags wear them out in public and feel it is a perfectly acceptable shirt to wear out for sushi. No one wants to see your hairy armpits while they stuff their faces with raw fish.

You wear your jeans below your ass and constantly have to pull them up to stop them from sliding further down your skinny little legs. This is seriously moronic behaviour. Why the hell would you wear your pants below your ass? Among other things, it makes you look like you've shit yourself when you wear your pants like that. It looks like you've taken a dump and the shit is weighing the seat of your pants down, dragging it well below where it should be, like a baby's drooping diaper.

If you wear your pants below your ass you're probably a lost cause, but if you want to get back on the path of righteousness, you can start by pulling your damn pants up to where they are supposed be worn, where real men wear them, above their asses. Cover up your boxer shorts, which are disgustingly visible at all times, because regardless of what your feeble mind thinks, nobody wants to see your skid marked undies as you walk down the street.

Apart from being cinched well below your ass, your jeans are also in-credibly tight at your ankles, coming to a halt right on top of your silly circus shoes. For some reason, you wear high tops with horrible colour schemes that used to be somewhat cool circa 1990 but haven't been cool for the past twenty years. What else can I say, you're a clown.

All in all, you look like a complete fool and scream douchebag loud and clear for all to hear. I suggest you burn all your clothes and start from scratch. This time when you go out shopping, do your best to avoid the douchebag depot for your clothing options. And put a fucking bend in your hat brim and wear it properly, straight off of your forehead like a normal man does. For God sakes, did you not have a father figure in your young life to ridicule you into looking like a normal man? Someone should have shamed and belittled you years ago. Had they done their job back then they may have spared you from the lonely existence you now lead in clown attire. Your daddy really let you down.

CHAPTER 19

THE INTELLIGENT IDIOT

You've unknowingly sat beside him on the train or on a couch at a party. Perhaps you have stood beside him in a store lineup or ordered a drink beside him at the bar. From the moment this moron laid his eyes upon you, he latched onto you like a hyena to a dying zebra's ass. As words suddenly spewed fast and furiously from his mouth, you looked up to the Lord above, with pain in your eyes, and asked what you had done to deserve such a fate.

With only one single breath of air, this douchebag can seemingly speak for an eternity without pause or need of a second breath. His brain functions so poorly, he probably doesn't need much oxygen anyway. Before you can even get a word of your own in edgewise and escape his vocal clutches, he's locked his tractor beam on to you and is not about to let go.

Words come out of his mouth with extreme ferocity. It would almost be amazing to witness if he wasn't such a total douchebag. As he spews verbal diarrhea like he has Norwalk virus of the voice box, you haven't the slightest clue what he is talking about. While he clearly thinks that he is clever, witty and intelligent, he is actually the complete opposite. He is fully and completely a moron, but he is his own biggest fan and, as far as you can tell, his only fan.

Even though he doesn't know you from Adam, he speaks to you with an incredible familiarity. He tries to impress you by using large and sophisticated words, but he most often says them incorrectly or uses them improperly. His incoherent babble contradicts itself from sentence to sentence - his tall tales spiraling quickly out of control from the get go. He is a man desperate for a friend, a stranger who tries far too aggressively to impress you and land you as his first and only friend.

With the social IQ of an autistic preschooler, he attempts to tell you jokes and asks you ridiculous questions, like if you've ever seen the inside of a spaceship (true story, that happened to me once — there are some fucked up people out there). But instead of pausing for a moment to let you answer, he answers his own questions and laughs at his own jokes for you. He doesn't need a partner to have a conversation, just like he doesn't need a partner to get laid. He does not dare let you get a word in edgewise, for he fears that if he ever leaves a break in his one sided conversation, you will take it as your opportunity to escape.

After a few moments in the presence of this douchebag, you fear that if you don't put a stop to his demented motor mouth almost immediately, you will be paying the price for the rest of the evening. It is at this point that you may be contemplating murder for the first time since exiting your vehicle from the freeway.

Everything this idiot says makes about as much sense as the jabbering verbalized hallucinations of a cracked out meth-head wandering the downtown streets at night. You wonder to yourself how someone this stupid could have made it this far through life without the constant supervision of a care aid. You are clearly not paying the slightest bit of attention to what this savant has to say, but that doesn't slow his prolific pace for a second.

When dealing with a douchebag like this, you have no choice but to walk away. Right in the middle of his never ending sentence, just turn foot and walk. It's the only move you can make to detach yourself from this human virus that won't land your ass in the slammer.

You've got to treat douchebags of this variety as if they were Band-Aids. You can't slowly peel them away. It's impossibly painful. Instead you've got to rip them right off in one fell swoop.

University Is Full of Them

I ATTENDED UNIVERSITY for one year when I was 18 years old. I went straight out of high school. The school I went to was a few hours' drive from where I grew up, so I moved away from home. I thought I'd have a great time being out on my own. However, in many ways it was probably the least fun year of my life.

I had a great time in high school. I was popular and got pretty good grades. I was good at sports, girls loved me (I'm incredibly handsome and remarkably humble, of course they loved me). There were also awesome parties to attend all the time. High school rocked!

It wasn't until I was partway through my first year of university that I realized why I hated it so much. I was surrounded by a plethora of nerds, many of whom tried too hard to portray that they were more intelligent and much cooler than they actually were. There were a lot of fake people around the school and I can't stand phonies.

I didn't have anything in common with most of the students I encountered at university. Granted, I was horribly misguided with regards to my course load and was enrolled in nothing that interested me in the slightest. While I was interested in girls, sports and partying, most people I encountered seemed to be interested in nothing but studying and playing video games on their computers.

I didn't live on campus that year, but the dorm room parties that I did attend were pretty lame. They were nothing like the parties that I was used to attending throughout my high school years, and certainly nothing like the frat house parties I'd seen in movies. Was Hollywood over-embellishing how awesome college parties could be? Impossible! I must have, simply, attended the wrong university. I mean, it's not like I was looking for an education. I was only 18 years old. I was looking for a good time.

The roommate that I had for my first semester was exactly the kind of guy I'm talking about. He was an engineering student, which probably says it all right there. From what I witnessed of the engineering students, they took being a nerd to a whole new level. They cranked the nerd nob all the way up to eleven!

While you have geeks in all faculties of a university, in no group will you find a bigger concentration of them than in the engineering department. If the Marine Corps are the best of the best, then the engineering students are the nerdiest of the nerds. (I realise now that not all engineers are enormous nerds, but at the time that's all I knew of them).

My roommate and his friends were prime examples. They were obsessed with computers and video games and, most shockingly to me, were completely oblivious to girls.

This roommate of mine had set up a long table on one wall of our living room that had three computers on it. That's right, three!

He would often have his fellow engineering friends over to play and sometimes they would even bring more computers with them. These computers weren't the tiny laptops of today either. This was over a dozen years ago now, so the computers were big, bulky things. They would hook them up together, I guess, and then spend hours playing weird games with each other. It was a sad and pathetic sight to behold. It was behaviour I would expect of a child, not of someone entering adulthood.

At first they invited me to join them, but they quickly gave up as they were nervous to approach me when I had a girl over, which I'm not going to lie, was as often as you'd expect of an 18 year old who was out on his on for the first time in his life. It's not that I have a severe aversion to video games or anything. I used to play video games a lot, when I was a kid, but they were all games that interested me – primarily sports and racing games. The games these guys were playing involved wizards, mythical creatures and all sorts of weird shit without much action involved.

While they were playing dragon games with each other, I was entertaining ladies, playing my guitar, watching hockey and football on TV and, of course, drinking beer - for I was still a growing boy and needed the calories. Not often was I ever playing video games. It just wasn't what I was into at the time.

There were a few occasions where I thought that I had the place to myself. I decided to have a girl over for a private evening. We would be on the couch, my female companion and I, well on the way to second base, or is it third base or... well, we were rounding the bases, when the front door would suddenly open and in would walk my roommate with three or four other social rejects in tow. Most often, the girl I was with would quickly put her top back on and jump off my lap, but depending on the girl, that may not have always been the case. Some chicks like to put on a show. I love women!

These university engineers, most of whom had never even touched a girl before, were shocked when they'd walk in and see a girl putting out. Their eyes would bug out of their heads as if they were cartoon characters. Too stupid to leave me alone though (as huge nerds have no idea how to abide by the bro code), after regaining the ability to control their limbs, they would set up shop at their computers in the living room and get lost, yet again, in their strange games. I would then be forced to take my lady-friend to my room in order to continue our private party out of site from any dragons, wizards or dudes with bad haircuts.

It was unbelievable how these guys could be so intelligent in some aspects - you can't become an engineer if you only possess half a brain - while at the same time be such morons when it came to life. I mean, some of them could figure out the most complex of physics problems yet couldn't understand how to do something as simple as microwaving instant oatmeal. This behaviour only became more obvious to me after my unwilling participation in many more nerd conventions.

Just for clarification, my housemate was not a bad guy, not at all. I liked him just fine and him and I got along well when it was just the two of us. We were just different people. A couple of his friends were, however, big nerdy douchebags whom I could hardly stand. They had no redeeming characteristics.

A month or so into the semester, a girl actually started tagging along with these geeks. I was told that she was in the engineering program as well, and like my roommate and his friends, she was coolest chick in the room.

This girl was, however, much better-looking than any of the guys. She wasn't quite as nerdy as any of them either. She wasn't smoking hot by any means, but she wasn't too bad, and as far as those nerds should have been concerned she should have been treated like a goddess. I mean let's be honest, she was female and she was paying attention to them. For possessing those two traits alone they should have worshipped the ground she walked on.

This she-engineer would, from then on out, also be at my place most of the time when my roommate and his buddies were there. She would hang out with them day and night, no matter how much they ignored her in favour of their computers. She was so desperate for their attention that, at times, it was rather sad. This poor girl so desperately wanted one of them to man-up and take her into the bedroom and have their way with her.

But none of them ever did, even though she was basically throwing herself at them day in and day out. It was as if they were asexual beings, completely uninterested in women and sex and only interested in monitors and keyboards. I mean, these guys never even watched TV. They just played on computers. They didn't seem human to me.

Because of the lady engineer's constant neglect, it quickly got to the point that if I was at home and without company, she would come over and join me in whatever I was doing. She'd pounce on over, sit on the couch beside me, ask me for a beer and chat my ear off while we watched a hockey game together.

Even though I wasn't sexually interested in her, I gave her the time of day. She was a nice girl and I felt sorry for her and her wasted efforts on the oblivious nerd herd. So, I paid attention to her, joked around with her and treated her well. I believe that her original intention in talking to me was to try to make one of the computer aficionados jealous by hanging out with me. She was trying to force at least one of them to ignore his video game and shed his attention in her direction.

Her efforts were never fruitful, at least not to my knowledge. It just blows my mind how anyone would care more about computers than about women. But these men exist and there are plenty of them out there, believe it or not, because I didn't believe it until I saw it first-hand.

On campus, it was nothing but more of the same. There were hordes of people that I had nothing in common with. The funny thing about university life is that it is the complete opposite of real life. While, to me, I was surrounded by scores of nerds, to them I was the outsider. I was not interested in computers or video games, science classes or hacky sack and, therefore, I was probably not 'cool' at university. It's some messed up shit there for those of you who have never been to a non-party school. That's what you get for going to a straight-laced university without any real big sports teams, I guess. I should have known better.

Now, I see some crazy colleges on TV, so not all schools could be as boring as the one I went to. That school in the movie *Animal House* looked pretty damn cool. There are some really great party schools, full of girls with loose morals who enjoy drinking copious amounts of beer on a regular basis. These are the same girls who will flash their tits at anyone with a camera. I wish I could have gone to one of those schools. Had I done so, I probably would have stayed longer -or perhaps I would have drank myself into a stupor and been smothered to death by a pair of giant breasts.

Needless to say, one year of that bullshit was enough for me. I was miserable and wanted no more of it. But I did learn something despite being absent from the majority of my classes. What I learned was that nowhere else on the entire planet will you find a higher concentration of intelligent idiots than on a university campus.

CHAPTER 20

HEY THERE, GREASEBALL

IT OOZES FROM his pores. It slicks back his hair. The grease excretion from this douchebag is like an out of control hazardous waste spill. He is so disgusting that the dollar bills pulled from his pocket are slimy. This supreme douchebag is known as the greaseball and he is a creature to be dealt with as if he were the plague. The problem is, that can be easier said than done, for the greaseball can be found anywhere you go, appearing when you least expect it.

He's that creepy guy at the bar, staring like a convicted pedophile at a group of young ladies. He's that guy making inappropriate comments at strangely inopportune times. He could be old or young. He could have long greasy hair or no hair at all.

He will be alone when spotted, because few others are desperate enough to be caught dead with this reject. But even though he is flying solo, he will act like he's the coolest guy around.

He's the life of the party, as far as he's concerned. He speaks far too familiarly with strangers. He'll try to interject himself into random conversations. He will try to draw attention to himself in any way he can. Perhaps it is by wearing an excessively loud and hideous shirt, or maybe it is by shouting ridiculous comments from the bar to the waitress, trying anything he can think of to get noticed.

This guy is so desperate for any type of attention or companionship, it's really quite sad. But you can't take pity on him. Pity will only encourage him to be the douchebag that he is and make him believe that his greaseball ways are acceptable. Pity gives him too much attention.

He should be ignored and avoided at all costs. If he gets a sense that you are someone that might give him the time of day, it's going to be harder to shake him than it was to shake that outbreak of herpes you picked up during Spring Break in Cancun. You can think of him as a predator whose prey is the weak and stupid.

As bad and disgusting as a greaseball can be, a greaseball with money is exponentially greasier. He aspires to get women to ignore his awkward and creepy social skills and his juvenile vocabulary by attempting to shift their focus and attention to his stack of cash.

This saturated douchebag will probably have a sports car. Odds are he won't really know how to drive it properly. He'll grind the gears and maybe even stall it out while taking a slow lap through the nightclub parking lot - a lap with the sole purpose of getting everyone waiting outside the nightclub to take notice.

Once he climbs out from his car, he is always seen with a wad of cash in his hand, being careful that the cash is always visible. Subtlety is most definitely not something the greaseball is familiar with.

He believes that the wad of cash in hand is all he needs to impress the ladies. The problem is that his douchebag behaviour is reinforced whenever he lands himself a catch. Every once in a while, he finds himself a tire-biter, a woman who wants nothing more in a man than for him to have cash that he is eagerly willing with which to depart.

This woman doesn't care how creepy, desperate or ugly the guy is. All she has her eyes on is his money. I guess in that sense, it's a bond made in heaven. He wants to get a woman any way he can and she wants to get money anyway she can, even if she has to perform dirty deeds to get it. Congratulations to them both. They deserve each other. I believe this is the premise on which all those *Real Housewives* television shows are based, and those are some special ladies.

Sometimes these greaseballs run in pairs. If you thought one of them alone was bad, two are exponentially worse. It's amazing to me that someone on Earth is able to put up with a greaseball douchebag. But it probably happens like this: One day, a greasy bastard encounters another and they hit it off. They share unproven pick-up lines and poorly invented war stories about parties and sexual conquests over women that never actually happened. Their legends grow as they banter back and forth like two young girls at a slumber party. Eventually, they become so enamoured with each other's legend that they develop into inseparable best friends.

Like Lloyd Christmas and Harry Dunne at a costume ball, but multiplied by ten, women feel as if they have been violated just by walking past these brainless idiots. Their incessant staring and perpetual rapist grins make them a stomach turning duo. Much like Donny and Marie, they are a sickening pair, as revolting as an incestuous couple.

The greaseball, more than any other person, fully embodies what it is to be a douchebag. From his hair to his clothing, his creepy looks and mannerisms to his desperate plays for women, he is a douchebag's douchebag. A human cockroach, if you will. At times he may scurry away and hide, but he will always be nearby, lurking in the dark, waiting for the perfect opportunity to pounce.

CHAPTER 21

THE INVERTED OREO

LOOK AT THAT GUY riding low, reclined back in his car, his straight-brimmed hat sitting crooked on his head. His arm is locked out straight, barely able to reach the steering wheel because his back rest is reclined to the max. A bandana is poking out of a black hat covered in gold-coloured Chinese symbols. He has a snarl on his face and is trying his best to look as intimidating as possible to all who pass him by. What a bad-ass! That guy is hardcore!

His shit-box of a car has been lowered so much that it comes to rest about an inch from the ground. It is so ridiculously close to the terrain below that it can easily become high-centered on a speed bump or small rock. The car is outfitted with rims that spin in the wind and a spoiler is attached to the trunk, even though the vehicle probably couldn't go from zero to sixty any faster than I could on a bicycle.

The strong sound of bass is blasting from his open windows as he listens to a comically bad gangster-rap album. The 'music' pounds so fe-rociously that it vibrates his car with each thump, almost loosening nuts and bolts right before his very eyes. He must think that the sound of a car's vibrating parts enhances the musical experience.

The stereo system in this douchebag's car is clearly more valuable than the car itself. It speaks a lot to a person's intelligence when the ac-cessories added to his car are more valuable than the car alone, especially if that car is worth no more than a few hundred dollars.

This douchebag is about as desperate for attention as a stripper with daddy issues and low self-esteem. He looks all around while sitting parked at the side of the road, hoping to notice people noticing him. If he does happen to meet eyes with a passer-by though, he looks at them menacingly, as if he were angry that they were noticing him. But the complete opposite is true, as nothing makes him happier than to be noticed.

You probably have a picture in your head of what this guy looks like by now, except there's one surprise, redneck. The guy I'm talking about is white as a ghost. I call him the inverted Oreo.

This douchebag tries to act as stereotypically inner-city black as he can. He takes every stereotype there is and he runs wild with it. He is very confused about his own identity and is so unintelligent that he tries to mimic the identity of some of society's worst. By doing so, he becomes the worst of the worst. He becomes society's excrement. This dude is the sediment that floated to the bottom of humanity's glass.

There's nothing more pitiful than someone trying to act as if they are someone they are not. Earlier in this book, I wrote about how much I dislike huge nerds who try to act like they are super cool, only to come off desperate and pathetic. The inverted Oreo is exactly the same and that makes him an enormous douchebag.

When not sitting in his car desperately trying to impress and intimidate, he shuts off the tunes and takes to the streets. This guy walks down the sidewalk with a fake limp and one arm stuck to the side of his body as if it were unable to move, while the other moves back and forth in exaggerated fashion. Every few steps he slows right down and moves his hand as if he's spinning an imaginary record in the air. Yes, he's an idiot.

On his head, a larger set of headphones he could not have. But he never wears them on his ears. They either sit really high on his head or around his neck, never where they are meant to be worn. Because of this placement, he has the volume cranked to maximum in order to hear the music.

Beneath the headphones there is a very large, fake gold chain wrapped around his little white pencil-thin neck. But it isn't just any old fake gold chain, this necklace has a very large medallion hanging from it in the shape of a dollar sign.

This retard will most likely also be wearing a sports jersey of some sort, even though he hates sports because he was always picked-on in grade school for being so bad at them. He has no loyalty to any sports team to justify wearing the jersey, but in his low double-digit IQ mind, he thinks wearing sports jerseys makes him cool because he has seen rappers wear them in music videos.

He tries to speak as if he comes from an inner city black ghetto, even though he was raised by middle-income parents in the suburbs. The dude basically speaks in Ebonics and puts on inner city black kid speech patterns and mannerisms. The boy is very confused and, thanks to his commitment to idiocy, a complete and utter douchebag.

Because of his foolish ways, he is not accepted by white or black people. He so desperately wants to be black, but is nothing but a joke and a poser to the black people he is trying to emulate, therefore they want nothing to do with him. He is such a useless tool, so unhappy with who and what he is, that no white people respect him either.

So he will continue to sit alone and listen to his angry gangster-rap all by himself in his lowered, 1994 Buick until he comes to the realization that the world hates him because he is a super-huge douchebag. Just because pretending to be an angry black man worked out for Eminem, doesn't mean anyone else should try it. The world most definitely does not need another Eminem.

CHAPTER 22

LOOK AT ME

I WANT TO MAKE money. I want to make lots of money. I want to be financially secure to the point where I never have to worry about paying the bills, ever again. Basically what I'm saying is that I've got nothing against money or people who have lots of it.

What I do have a problem with are those douchebags that have a lot of money and flaunt it in everyone's face with every chance they get.

The Fancy Pants Restaurant Douchebag

THIS IS A GUY THAT, within five seconds of meeting him, you want to trip face down into a mud puddle. He's the guy that pulls up to the valet parking spot outside of a high class downtown restaurant in his Jaguar and is unable to open his own car door. After he shuts off his engine, Mr. Perfect waits for the parking valet to come over and open his door for him.

Once out of his car, this gold-plated loser will not give assistance to his lady in the passenger seat. Instead, he will also wait for the valet to assist with her door.

This wealthy douchebag will not smile or thank the valet for his assistance. Instead, he will wave money in the air for all those around to see before handing it to the valet. With his exaggerated display of tip-giving, he is trying to say, 'Look world, look at what a generous man I am.

Admire me. That's right, this is a five-dollar bill. This peasant valet probably only makes five dollars an hour. Therefore, I have single-handedly doubled his hourly salary. I am a wonderful man! Cherish me.' Puke.

Witnessing this man as he makes his way slowly towards the restaurant with a pompous gait, you may find yourself wondering what it is that's stuck up his asshole. Maybe he misplaced some of his five dollar bills up there? Maybe it's some gold bullion? Stranger things have happened.

Most likely this guy will be wearing some type of clothing that will draw attention to him and let you know that he has money to spend. So there is a good chance he will be wearing a two thousand-dollar suit with alligator shoes and cashmere socks or some shit like that. Maybe he's wearing some platinum encrusted underwear? Who knows?

To add to it all, the lady in his presence most certainly will be displaying a wealth of money on her person as well. Perhaps she is wearing a very large and plush fur coat. Perhaps it is the number of ridiculously expensive name brands she is visibly displaying on her person, or the plethora of diamonds strangling her neck that are used to illustrate wealth.

The wealthy douchebag's head is always on a swivel, constantly scanning his surroundings to see if people are looking at him with impressed and envious eyes. Walking from the car to the restaurant, it is amazing that he does not fall flat on his face, for he is looking everywhere except where he is going.

Approaching the front door of the restaurant, this fool will do all he can to not open his own door. He believes, wholeheartedly, that a man of his social stature should never have to open any door.

Therefore, if a doorman is not present, he will often allow another patron to open the door, and swoop in under the patron's arm as if he were only there to open the door for the douchebag.

This happened to me once, I kid you not. Surprisingly, the words 'Thank you' were not even muttered as he weaseled his way past my armpit and into the restaurant.

Once inside, the wealthy douchebag makes it immediately clear to all around that he is by far the most important person in the room. The hostess may be involved with another dinner party, but no matter, for the wealthy douchebag will butt his way in most intrusively and interrupt the other party in order to receive immediate service.

Upon being seated at his table, he will examine the wine list and then tell his date, while speaking loud enough so that anyone within twenty feet of him can clearly hear, that he has found the perfect wine to start the extravaganza. He will go into great detail describing the wine, as many a douchebag is fond of doing, speaking to its country of origin, the type of grape used, the flavour, bouquet and whatever other bullshit drivel he can throw in there in an attempt to impress.

Then he will raise his voice even louder when mentioning the most important thing about the wine, the preposterously high price, and will say something asinine like, 'It is listed here at five hundred dollars per bottle, which is well worth it for the superior quality of wines from that region.' If only lightning could strike him down right there and put the other restaurant patrons out of their misery. But the world is never that kind to those in need.

Upon the arrival of the waiter, with the excessively overpriced wine in hand, the wealthy douchebag will put on another 'look at how great and impressive I am' show for all. Once the waiter pours his first taste and awaits his impression - holy shit - sit back and wait to be impressed.

I don't often order a bottle of wine in restaurants, but whenever I have, I have always felt like an idiot when the waiter pours a little from the bottle and waits for my approval. That is because I never want to swirl the wine around in my glass and be forced to sample it and give my opinion. I'm not a wine snob. I just like drinking the stuff. I haven't received a university degree in wine sampling. I'm not a sommelier. And let's be honest, once the waiter has popped the cork and I've taken a sample, am I really going to tell him that I hate the wine and spit it out into my glass and demand a new and different bottle? I don't think so. Wasting perfectly good hooch is alcohol abuse. The way I see it is that I bought it and he opened it, therefore I'm drinking it.

But the wealthy douchebag takes great joy in this process. He sees it as a superb opportunity to dazzle all around with his vast knowledge of wine, a subject he thinks others will find impressive.

Therefore, once the waiter has poured him his small sample glass, the douchebag will spend a thorough amount of time examining the product. First, he holds the wine up to the light while swirling it in his glass. Next will come a ridiculous comment about the wine's appearance or the way the light refracts from its hue. It is at this point that everyone around will be praying for the man to spill the red wine all over his starched white shirt. Not to finish the performance too quickly, he will then place the glass back down onto the table for some more swirling.

Next, it's on to the 'bouquet,' for all men of his nature have to make good use of the small handful of French words they actually retain. If you haven't been impressed yet by his performance, perhaps his usage of a French word or two will win you over, if he hasn't already.

Next, the dip shit will bury his nose in the glass and take in a large, exaggerated breath of wine odor not once, not twice, but thrice and then, after a long and pronounced pause, announce his findings. Coincidentally, he rattles off the exact description of the bouquet that he read in the menu and was told by the waiter when he ordered the wine.

Next comes the long-anticipated tasting. Oh how everyone has been waiting with baited breath for the tasting. The waiter has only been waiting for a full minute by this point and isn't at all pissed off about it. He certainly doesn't have any other tables to tend to.

The wealthy douchebag finally feels that he's put on a big enough show and is now ready to put the damn stuff in his big, loud mouth. But not even this process can he hurry. Instead of just taking a swallow he, instead, swishes the wine around in his cheeks, for a small eternity, before finally swallowing. As he does so, he closes his eyes as if to heighten his already keen sense of taste.

After making the waiter stand idly by for a sufficient amount of time, the moron finally gives the waiter a nod of approval, allowing him to fill both glasses. By this point in time, I'm sure the waiter would love to do nothing more than to pour the contents of the bottle all over the pompous man's head before smashing the bottle on his face as a finale. But he refrains. Bravo, to the performance though, bravo!

Now that the wine spectacle has come to an end, it's time to move on to the menu. The only reason this douchebag is looking at the menu is to find the most expensive dishes. He doesn't really care what he eats, he merely wants to find grand, extravagant dishes with which to impress all, including the woman he is sitting with.

If there happens to be a gaudy tower of expensive seafood on the menu, that is what he will order. If an endangered species is available, then that will suffice. The wealthy douchebag is nothing if not predictable.

During dinner, this first-class asshole will gloat and brag about his many exotic trips. He also can't help himself but to mention all the famous people he's had the chance of seeing. There is no evidence to prove available to prove his truthfulness, so the sky is the limit for his stories of celebrity interactions. Patrons sitting anywhere near this man have long since grown tired and are now certainly praying that he will take in a sufficient breath during one of his tall tales to inhale a large piece of crab meat and succumb to chocking. Of course, no one in the restaurant is that lucky. A patron, instead, decides to key the douchebag's Jaguar on the way back to his Ford pickup. Justice is served.

I Wait For Nothing

THE WEALTHY DOUCHEBAG does not thrive well outside of his co-cooned world. If ever he happens to find himself in situations unnatural to him, also known as the real world, he unravels faster than Charlie Sheen in a Las Vegas brothel. Now, I've never been to a brothel with Charlie Sheen – although it has always been a dream of mine – but I would imagine that things would come undone in a hurry.

The wealthy douchebag is not accustomed to coping in the real world and is most certainly not accustomed to waiting for anything. Whenever he goes out shopping or to restaurants, he is usually dealt with promptly, as he is known for dropping copious amounts of cash. People wait on him hand and foot, and as a result he is not accustomed to having to do anything for himself. The man is always surrounded by people that will do his bidding for him and he is seldom forced to wait in line. He has peasants on staff to wait in lines for him.

That is why when the wealthy douchebag is forced to wait for anything, such as to see the doctor in the Emergency Room, he quickly becomes enraged. Not receiving the most prompt of service can make him flip his lid and lose his mind. Because of his superiority complex, he becomes almost instantly angered when treated in the same fashion as the inferior people that walk the earth with him.

If he is not seen to almost immediately by a nurse or physician in the ER, he will throw a temper tantrum just like that of a small, ill-disciplined child. I have born witness to this type of behaviour before. It was a sad and pathetic sight. I once witnessed a man raise his voice, scream of injustices and demand to be seen before any other hospital patient, even though many of those around him were quite obviously much sicker or much more seriously injured than he was. Many around him were so bad off that they would have been unable to raise their voices and complain about anything at all. But that was of no concern to the wealthy douchebag, because to him, all other people are but second-class citizens.

While his asshole-like behaviour may work for him in certain places or under certain circumstances, in places such as hospitals, his rotten behaviour will do nothing but backfire. You don't want to piss off the people who are there to help you. They will feel that you are ungracious and will not be willing to show you the respect that you think you deserve. If you're sick enough to holler, you're not sick enough to be seen and treated first.

In the hospital, the sicker or more injured you are, the more sympathy you will garner from staff and therefore the quicker you will be helped. If, however, you are healthy enough to yell and complain and basically piss off all the staff - not to mention all the patients around you - you will be ignored for as long as the staff can get away with it.

No one wants to help an ungrateful, irate and egomaniacal douchebag. So this man with more money than brains will be waiting an awful long time, much longer than he would have waited had he just kept his big yap shut. And the self-inflicted neglect will, at some point, send him into another state of blind rage, and it will be glorious.

An incident like this is a much needed reality check for the wealthy douchebag. Being a rich asshole doesn't always get you what you want.

There are certain times and places where the size of your wallet won't help you out one little bit. Sometimes a little patience and kindness can go a long way.

The wealthy douchebag is a true injustice in this world. For of all the people who would be good people and perform good deeds with their money were they lucky enough to earn a fortune, a fortune has instead found its way to this inconsiderate human waste, a man who does nothing with his money but hoard it to himself and flaunt it in the faces of others. He has never helped an unfortunate soul with his money and he never will. If you ever have an opportunity to screw with a wealthy douchebag, take it. Nothing makes me happier than seeing an obnoxious douchebag suffer.

CHAPTER 23

CRITICIZE THIS

WE LIVE IN A TIME of criticism. From tabloid row at the grocery store checkout isle to the demented and distorted 'news' on Fox News Channel, many headlines these days seem to be about nothing more than criticizing the actions, exploits and creativity of others.

These sources often pride themselves on discrediting wonderful people who actually create and achieve. I find that to be morally reprehensible. We live in a culture where it would appear as if the majority of people feel the constant need to stand on their internet soap boxes and criticize the minority of people who actually have thoughts and ideas of their own. Social media has given a voice to a great number of people who should never be heard, much like a Japanese karaoke bar. Facebook has become the world's karaoke bar. Thanks a lot, Zuckerberg.

I don't wish to rid the earth of all critics. Certain critics can aid us through the decision making process of everyday life. Sometimes they are a necessary evil. Sometimes they are not evil at all.

Professional movie or food critics can help people decide what movie they might want to watch or what new restaurant they'd like to eat at. Sure, some of them are probably tyrants and I'm sure movie studios, chefs and restaurant owners hate some of these critics to the core of their beings. Regardless, they do still serve a purpose.

Gainfully employed and useful critics aside, why are so many members of society desperate to criticize those whom are better than them? Whether it be criticizing a professional athlete for passing instead of shooting or criticizing the President of the United States every single time he makes a decision (for the love of God they can't all be wrong), there is an overabundance of haters and criticizers in the world today.

As much as I hate hearing the opinions of the half-baked haters of life, they are becoming increasingly difficult to escape. I'm bombarded with useless opinions every time I turn on the TV or radio, when I go to work, or when I stand in the checkout line at the grocery store.

There are so many so-called celebrities nowadays that are famous for nothing other than being famous. Regardless, they are worshipped by the masses. Multitudes of morons hang onto every word they have to say as if it were gospel. Many of these 'celebrities' appear to be borderline retarded. Yet they are interviewed incessantly and are always being asked for their thoughts and opinions on topics broad and narrow. There is nothing I enjoy more than listening to the illogical ramblings of a half-witted social icon.

Cameras follow these people around everywhere they go, even though they have no apparent talents or redeeming qualities to speak of, other than maybe a nice pair of tits or an ass that just won't quit. So many people these days have a misguided and irrational need to hear the feeble-minded thoughts and opinions of these pseudo-celebrities. Then the kicker is that after watching these fools on television, many celebrity worshipers will feel the need to criticize those they apparently idolize. That's an unstable love-hate relationship right there. Sometimes I am embarrassed of being a human being.

Dumbass social media fanatics aside, the mainstream media are the biggest proponents of the criticism epidemic, especially stations like Fox News Channel. That organization is full of nothing but angry, opinionated douchebags who contribute nothing to society other than to spew hate-filled criticisms of, what are quite often, very good, caring and intelligent people. But at Fox News if you can't be smarter, just be louder. Everyone knows that the loudest guy in the room is always rightest guy in the room.

It could be a new presidential policy or a new and clever book written by an incredibly handsome man. Wait a second, I think a book like that just so happens to be in your hands right now. Either way, the angst-filled television journalists, with their not-so-hidden agendas, will rip them apart as they see fit, regardless of the merits of the actual work they are criticizing.

I had my inaugural taste of critics when my first book, *Let Me Put My Poems In You,* hit the shelves a few years back (which, because I am an overgrown 12 year old, was published under the pen name *Matty Cox*). The book was reviewed by a few newspapers and most of them understood what I was trying to do. The book is nothing but hilarious, mindless and inappropriate poems. If you have no greater expectations than that when reading the book, you'll love it.

Most of the reviews I received were good, save for one newspaper where the author of the article was clearly a straight-laced and uptight dude absent of a sense of humour. All reviewers who didn't have sticks up their posteriors wrote such things as, 'Move over William Shakespeare – there's a new Bard in town,' or 'five stars in the category of sexual euphemisms' – my personal favourite - or even '*Let Me Put My Poems in You* is a great choice for a college kid's coffee table or bathroom book. No matter which page one chooses to open, that poem is sure to garner a laugh.'

But one particular laugh assassin didn't get me or my book at all. I don't take myself seriously. Maybe it's a character flaw, but it's who I am. All I want to do is write things and do things that make people laugh provide entertainment. If you don't like what I do, shed a few brain cells to get down to my level, loosen up and you'll love me (holy shit do I ever have a big ego). I'd prefer to make everyone laugh, but if that doesn't happen I'm not going to lose too much sleep over it.

The title of my detractor's article was: *Roses are Red, Let Me Put My Poems In You Sucks.* Honestly, that's like saying the Naked Gun movies are awful. Of course they're awful if you are comparing them to Oscar winning dramatic movies. But if you take them at face value, take them for the light hearted, hilarious non-sense that they are intended to be, you will love them. They will make you laugh.

In an attempt at putting me down, the author of the article wrote such things as, 'Cox is like a 12-year-old with the vocabulary of a 25-year-old -- he's able to articulate the perverted and juvenile thoughts of a junior high student with voice of someone much older, but also more profane.' I can't argue with that. I'll take it!

While I may think the author of that article was a bit of a douchebag for taking himself too seriously, at least he was criticizing something that was sent to him by my publisher for the sole purpose of being critiqued. Regardless, if I agree with what he wrote or not, at least he was just doing his job. But the writers of the numerous magazines and television shows who go out of their ways to find people and things to unnecessarily criticize take things much too far.

Sadly, the general public condones this behaviour by continually tuning in to watch spite-driven shows or by purchasing brain-dead magazines by the crate. As a society, we need to stop watching those awful shows and stop buying mindless celebrity gossip magazines. Instead, read proper books. Watch good television (if in doubt there's always sports), and form an opinion or two about the world that didn't come from some soulless and idiotic pseudo-celebrity. And please, whatever you do, don't share those opinions with the rest of us unless you can at least write a complete sentence and form a complete and coherent thought. That is the very least you could do to help slow the regression of society.

The Desk Athlete

I LOVE PLAYING sports and I love watching them. What can I say: there is a lot of testosterone coursing through these veins, and more than likely a little scotch. While I can, at times, be as much of a culprit of professional sports criticism as any other man, I usually quite good at toning it down. I will often catch myself and realize how goofy it is for me to be criticizing the abilities of someone who is better than I am at their respective sport. It's one thing to criticize an athlete for blowing all his money at the casino or for complaining that the millions of dollars he already makes aren't enough for playing a game that children play on weekends, but to criticize him strictly on his athletic ability is a little silly.

I mean honestly, if I knew how to be a better quarterback than Tom Brady, wouldn't I be in the NFL? If I knew how to kick a ball better than David Beckham ever did, wouldn't I be making millions of dollars to play soccer?

I can't call every Monday morning quarterback a douchebag, because that's just not the case, far from it. Every sports fan likes to throw in his two cents, and there's nothing wrong with that. That's one of the great things about sports. Talking about sports with your buddies and co-workers can be cathartic.

I guarantee this is nothing new. I'm sure if you could go way back in time to the day after the world's first ever sporting event, you would find a group of men standing around a cave discussing what they would have done differently had they themselves been kicking the rock. It's only natural for men to have an unrealistically high opinion of their own athletic abilities and knowledge. It's just the way we were made.

The real douchebag in the world of sports' criticism is known as the sports know-it-all. If you are like me, when you are in the presence of the sports know-it-all it takes every bit of your will power to not choke him unconscious each and every time he opens up that big yap of his.

The sports know-it-all is as opinionated as they come. He may work with you, he may be a friend of a friend, or he may be that sports radio personality that you just can't stand. Every time his show comes on the air, you wonder to yourself who the hell ever made the executive decision to put a microphone in front of this guy. Then you quickly change the station. Ah, Katy Perry....much better.

This guy is all business when it comes to his professional sports criticism. He never jokes around while talking sports. There is no light-heartedness about him. He is extremely serious, unable even to so much as crack a smile while talking sports. That personality trait makes him an insufferable douchebag.

Even though he is most likely an extremely un-athletic statistics nerd, he would have you believe that he knows how to play every sport to perfection. He knows what is wrong with every athlete and how they could perform better in any given situation. This sports savant even seems to know what a particular player should have done alternatively in a certain situation - one that cost his favourite hockey team the game. All of this knowledge he possesses, even though the only time in his life that he's ever laced up the skates, his father had to tie them for him.

While Georges St Pierre won most of his fights without getting so much as a scratch on him, the sports know-it-all douchebag shares his immense knowledge with all those he encounters about how Georges could have done better in each specific fight, or what submission he should have pulled at the end of the third round to finish his opponent. The man has gone so far as to have memorized a dictionary of fight terminology and uses as many terms as he possibly can, as frequently as possible, to try to impress. He has, essentially, become a human thesaurus of fighting. He does all of this even though he has never spent one minute of his life inside the confines of a fight gym, not to mention inside the ring. He couldn't actually perform one of the moves he so proudly describes in great detail, even if he were forced to at gunpoint.

While he takes his criticisms as seriously as a bad case of hemorrhoids, you can't help but laugh your ass off that this pathetic little pencil neck geek is giving, of all things, fighting advice. I mean, this guy is so skinny and uncoordinated that, were even the slightest of men to pick a fight with him, he would most likely shit himself silly with fear. The dude probably couldn't fight his way out of a wet paper bag. Yet he proclaims, to all who will hear him out, that he knows the fight game better than the world's greatest fighters. He, certainly, does not have the eye of the tiger. I pity the fool.

CHAPTER 24

THE NIGHTCLUB REGULAR

LIKE A CAST member of defunct *Jersey Shore*, the nightclub regular is a douchebag's douchebag. He, most likely, still lives at home with his parents, having converted a portion of their basement into a greasy douchebag den, equipped with posters of hip hop artists and John Travolta in bellbottoms. If, through some sort of miracle, he no longer lives at home, he most likely shares a house or an apartment with several other people, earning just enough money to pay his small portion of rent by working a part-time job at a fast food kiosk in the mall.

The nightclub regular is obsessed with doing arm curls and abdominal crunches at the gym. He spends as much time at the gym as he does at his part-time job. His goal at the gym is not to become strong or healthy. Working on any muscle group other than his biceps and abdominals would be a waste of time for this winner. He works out for one reason and on reason only: to get chicks. To this guy, women are clearly only interested in biceps and six-pack abs. He must believe that woman love nothing more than men with uneven body types, men like himself, who have big arms and tiny legs. It's an attractive look.

His arms bulge out of his extra tight tee-shirts, but his skinny little legs don't even fill out the slim-fitting pants he wears. But he never looks far enough down in the mirror to notice his legs. He is obsessed with his face, arms and stomach, unconcerned about anything else. All that matters are if his biceps are big enough to impress a drunken Paris Hilton clone at the nightclub.

Aside from his love of biceps curls, this douchebag also has a penchant for tattoo parlours. Name an ugly and cliché tattoo of the douchebag, I guarantee you he's got it, or at the very least is saving his pennies for it. He is a firm believer in tattoo power. Tattoo power, for those who are unaware, is a belief that the more tattoos you have on your body, the tougher you inherently are.

That must be why his arms and legs are covered with a random mess of tattoos, each ink blotch indistinguishable from the next. His body looks like he let an intoxicated Maori warrior go nuts with needles and ink. Regardless, this idiot thinks he looks super badass.

When not 'getting inked or pumping the guns,' this douchebag's spare time is divided evenly between self-grooming and nightclub attendances. The nightclub regular spends more time grooming before a night out than a high school girl does before her prom.

He plucks and shapes his eyebrows with obsession, to the point where they don't even resemble any naturally occurring shape or form. The edges are too straight and the hair is buzzed far too short. When he's out in public, people stare at him because he looks like a freak. In his douchebag mind though, the staring strangers exist because he looks so good. This, unfortunately, provides the positive reinforcement he needs to continue his misguided and ridiculous grooming habits.

If the nightclub regular is able to grow a beard, there is a good chance he will have a thinly landscaped beard, one that no real man would ever be caught dead wearing. It must take him hours a day to shave such a precise diagram onto his face, let alone to maintain all his other grooming habits. It is clearly time well spent as far as this misguided man is concerned. I mean, he probably got laid last month by a highly inebriated and slightly attractive female, and from his point of view, his hours spent grooming and pumping his biceps probably had everything to do with it. The half-dozen appletinis had nothing to do with it.

After a couple hours of preparation, the nightclub regular is finally ready to go. He will instinctively know which bar to attend depending on what night of the week it is. The decision will be based on what club has the cheapest drink specials, because the cheaper the drinks, the drunker, and therefore, the sluttier, some women will become. He can't afford to buy ladies drinks at ten or twenty bucks a pop, but if it's one-dollar highball night, well then it's game on. Go get 'em, big spender!

Smooth Entry

THE NIGHTCLUB regular's typical night at the bar goes a little something like this:

He strolls into the club as if he owns the place, his head held high and chest proud as he struts past the steroid-injected doorman and into the bar. He has his head is on a swivel as he scouts the place for 'talent,' a word straight out of the douchebag dictionary. All normal dudes look for women: douchebags look for 'talent.'

The douchebag makes his way to the bar and asks the bartender for 'the usual.' The bartender then looks at him with a confused look on his face and asks, 'What's the usual?' The nightclub regular has such an overly inflated ego (a safety mechanism to try to mask his extreme lack of self-confidence) that in his own mind, he is king shit. He, therefore, assumes that because he has previously ordered a drink from that particular bartender sometime in the past, he would have made such a good impression that the bartender would have been unable to forget about him or his drink order.

With a drink now in hand, the nightclub regular finds a seat that allows him a good vantage point of the entire bar. After circling the table for a minute, he sits down and spreads his arms and legs out wide, taking up as much space as he possibly can.

Sitting there with a creepy looking grin on his face, women whisper remarks to each other as they walk by. Most women are obviously disgusted by this creepy weirdo, but he is immune to all ill appraisals. All attention is good attention.

He eventually spots some prey from his perch and quickly decides to move in for the kill, before his victim can flutter away. As if he believes he possesses all the charm of George Clooney at a cocktail party, he approaches the unfortunate lady with the misguided swagger and confidence of a lion.

Brushing up beside her, he immediately invades her personal space. Before he has even opened his mouth, the lucky girl's smile has disappeared from her face and transformed into a look of disgust. She has also adjusted her body language to put out a vibe that now says 'go to hell.' Women are amazing at that.

Completely incapable of reading even the most obvious of social cues, the nightclub regular throws out one of his studied greaseball pickup lines, something like: 'I hear your ankles are having a party. Want to invite your pants down?' To which the lady cannot reply because of all the vomit that has filled her mouth in response.

If the look of disgust on the woman's face wasn't obvious before, it has sure become so by that point. She turns away from him, abruptly, flipping her hair in his face. However, the sleazy douchebag remains unfazed.

Not easily discouraged, he walks around to the other side of his poor victim so that he is once again face to face with her. He spews another putrid pickup line. This time she lets out a sigh of disgust and tells him to take a hike. He merely takes her actions as an invitation to pursue her with even more vigor.

The moron offers to buy her a drink and she again tells him to go away. He does not leave but says to her that he likes it when women play hard to get. At this point, the poor woman is probably wondering why she left her pepper spray at home for the evening.

Still unfazed, he once again offers to buy her a drink. The victim finally comes to her breaking point and has no choice but to raise her voice and yell at him: 'Leave me alone, you freak! I don't want one of your roofie-coladas!'

With great reluctance, he finally admits defeat. He turns to leave her alone, but not before spouting a pathetic parting phrase like: 'You'll regret that decision when you go home alone tonight, gorgeous.' She would gladly go home alone for a hundred years than go home once with him.

Off to abuse yet another woman with his mere presence, the nightclub regular's evening has only begun. He will try a similar approach with several other women, always ending with the same result of immediate rejection. No amount of rejection, however, can remove the creepy douchebag smile from his soul crushing face. He is so demented that even the hostile attention he receives makes him happy. Some attention is better than no attention.

If you know someone like the reject I am describing, disown him immediately. He's got to hit rock bottom before he will ever change his douchebag ways. If you're not willing to abandon him - perhaps he is your son and you still have faint hope - the least you can do is to arrange an intervention. Hide all of his razors, creams, lotions, tweezers, perfumes and body sprays and cancel his gym membership. He will have a nervous breakdown, but he needs it. You've got to break someone before you can fix him.

CHAPTER 25

MOB MENTALITY

WHY IS IT THAT society so often seems to live down to the lowest common denominator, especially when assembled together in large public gatherings? Good people become outnumbered by the degenerate and then the good take a hike and the degenerate douchebags are left behind to take control.

The feeble minded masses also remain behind, too stupid to leave when decent and smart people bow-out. Those feeble-minded individuals are very easily manipulated. Like bees to clover they are attracted to douchebag behaviour and will blindly follow suit.

It starts with one retard thinking that it's cool to light a trash can on fire. The next thing you know, another equally dull-witted creature follows suit. Yet another knucklehead witnesses the act, thinks it would also make him cool in the eyes of his equally intellectually-deficient spectators were he to participate, and decides to light something on fire himself. And so it begins.

The more profound the level of IQ deficiency, the more willing one is to participate in, and escalate, a senseless riot. I'm going to go out on a limb here and suggest that you wouldn't find many scientists or scholars participating in a meritless riot. I'm willing to bet that, of all those arrested in the aftermath of a pointless riot, not one of the willing participants would be a highly educated or highly intelligent human being. Even when drunk out of my mind, I still have more functioning brain cells than the degenerate douchebags that participate in riots.

I'm not suggesting that there are never instances in life that call for public uprisings. Sometimes rioting is the only way for oppressed members of a society to stand up, band together and fight for their rights.

Government oppression in many countries around the world is so severe that only a large coup d'état can begin to change the injustices. Many governments around the world have been guilty of oppressing, enslaving and even murdering their own people. This type of horrible behaviour has, at times, led to uprisings by the oppressed.

Public demonstrations and even rioting can occur as a last measure taken by beaten-down people to let their government, not to mention the world, know that they are fed up with what is going on. It's a gesture to show that they are not going to take the abuse any longer.

But I'm not writing a book about people who need to fight for their rights. I'm writing a book about douchebags, like those who riot not because of severe government injustices or oppression, but merely because they feel like it. Those who riot because they were bored or had nothing better to do. I'm talking about people who riot for no purpose and with no objective in mind, other than wanting to destroy property, loot and steal, merely because the opportunity arises.

The people who rioted in Vancouver after the Vancouver Canucks Game Seven loss to the Boston Bruins in the Stanley Cup Final a handful of years back are precisely the douchebags to whom I am referring. The participating degenerates did nothing but reinforce the already poor opinion that I have of society in general.

The home team lost the game and walked away empty-handed. Big deal. It happens. C'est la vie. I was a fan and I didn't riot. There's always next year.

But I don't think that most of the rioters really gave a shit about a hockey game. Many came downtown with the intent on rioting well before the game had even begun, not to mention before the outcome had been decided. The other losers who participated in the riot merely saw an opportunity arise and decided to join in on the fun. What the hell? Why not?

I don't know about the rest of you, but when I'm getting ready to go out and watch a game, incendiaries are not among the belongings I pack with me. I'm not wandering around the house as I prepare to leave saying shit like, 'Okay, I've got my wallet, my keys and my phone. Good. Oh, I almost forgot! Hey, honey! Honey! Do you know where I left those Molotov cocktails? And where's my gasmask? Got me some cop cars to burn down tonight! When the riot police show up I don't need that teargas stinging my eyes.'

The reason I don't pack shit like that with me when heading out is because I am not an imbecile. I don't need to cause unnecessary trouble. I don't need to fight for no reason. I will only fight if a fight is necessary, if there is something worth fighting for. Exuding mob mentality and joining in on a riot, for no other reason than because your partially developed brain thinks it would be fun and exciting, makes you a massive douchebag, a real big piece of society's trash.

While people in other countries around the world have rioted for worthwhile and legitimate reasons, the Vancouver riot was nothing but douchebags being douchebags. It was as if an angry hoard of brain-damaged gorillas had escaped from the zoo and had taken to the streets.

While other governments in other countries have enticed riots by doing such things as senselessly killing their own people, the city of Vancouver did nothing of the sort. What those in charge of the city did do, however, was throw a party for everyone to enjoy. They wanted the people of the city to come downtown to watch Game Seven of the Stanley Cup Finals. So I guess it's the city's fault.

The municipal government did a good and decent thing for the city of Vancouver. They wanted everyone to get into the spirit of sport and camaraderie. People clearly missed the point. I doubt the government will ever do something like that for the people of Vancouver again, at least not any time soon. Although, governments seem to have absolutely no hindsight, so the riots may not affect anything.

The city erected enormous projection screens and closed off a few downtown streets to vehicle traffic so that large crowds could gather and watch the game unfold. Vancouver threw a party for its citizens, and what did some of the citizens do to say thank you? They started a riot.

Before the game had even concluded, several people began flipping cars over and setting them on fire. No cars were sacred, as a few police cars were flipped over and set aflame, as well as civilian cars. Any vehicle unfortunate enough to be parked near the mob was targeted.

Dozens of garbage cans were also set on fire. Some idiots even tried to burn down buildings, throwing Molotov cocktails through store front windows. Other people were dancing around like drunken fools on top of burning vehicles and broken-down fences.

The news cameras even filmed a couple of good buddies as they urinated, side by side, onto a burning vehicle that had been flipped onto its roof. It must have been a really romantic moment for those two morons to share. They represented their city well. I'm sure their friends and families are proud of them. Mama was probably tickled pink to observe that behaviour while watching the news from home.

By this point in the riot, clouds of teargas were filling the streets. The teargas didn't disperse the crowds as the police had intended, though, for a part because some of the enthusiastic rioters had come prepared with their own gasmasks. I don't even know where I could find a gasmask.

Others had covered their faces with their shirts. Some of the rioters would even kick canisters of teargas back in the direction of the police officers who fired them. Those were some brave little fuckers, weren't they? I mean, kicking an inanimate canister a few feet in front of you sure proves that you are a tough bastard. An action like that must surely strike fear into the souls of cops, far and wide.

One cop got himself a small victory that was caught on camera when he fired a teargas canister from his grenade launcher and struck one of the active rioters directly in the groin. Upon impact to the scrotum, the douchebag dropped like a ton of bricks and teargas almost immediately engulfed him. It was hilarious. Nut shots always bring the laughs.

Watching from my couch as I saw that idiot take a direct shot to the sack, I nearly fell to the floor in a fit of laughter. I could hardly breathe. It was priceless. Hopefully the trauma from the canister was enough to prevent the man from ever procreating. The world would definitely be better off without any of that useless dude's offspring plaguing it.

As the riot ensued and gathered momentum, many of the participants began throwing large objects through shop windows. Those actions allowed others to enter, vandalize and loot the insides of the stores. News cameras were right there in the thick of it, front and center, filming people as they exited smashed store fronts with stolen goods in hand and smiles on their faces. Many of these knuckle draggers didn't even attempt to hide from the cameras. It's going to be hard to argue a defense for that one in court.

Watching it all unfold on television, I saw a man assault a woman while a TV network's high-definition cameras filmed him in action, capturing his face clear as day for all of us at home to see. The idiot assaulted this woman even though two cops were directly in front of him. One of the cops was holding a video camera that he had pointed straight at the degenerate's face as well. Clearly some people's parents didn't do a good enough job raising them.

As stupid as you have to be to participate in a pointless and senseless riot, you have to be that much dumber to do so knowing full well that you are being recorded. Several different television networks had their cameras out, recording all the action. Not only that, but many of the riot police were carrying video cameras with them as well, recording the faces of all the members in the crowd that they encountered.

As if all that potential video evidence were not enough, let's not forget that we live in the digital age. Every other idiot out there in that riot had his camera phone out, taking pictures of himself, his friends, and everyone else who was participating. People were mugging for the camera harder than a desperate, has-been, D-list celebrity on a reality television show. Never before in my life have I seen such a large gathering of douchebags. It was an embarrassment to watch.

A good percentage of the rioting fools were so clearly brain-damaged that they even posted photos of their exploits on their own Facebook pages later that night when they got home. Many of these photos depicted their own participation in such events as looting, vandalism and the burning of private property and police cars. These incompetent douchebags were bragging to everyone they knew, in person and online, about their endeavours. No sense in trying to keep your criminal activities a secret so as to not get caught. It's unbelievable to me just how willing so many people are to be their own worst enemies.

It may be sad, but no matter how much I may hope for the opposite, douchebags always seem to live down to the low expectations that I set for them. If I sound like I have a negative opinion of society, that's because I do. Society never fails to reinforce my negative beliefs. The scum seldom seem to fail to drag others down to their level. People are too often willing to succumb to idiocy. The bar is already set so low and they just drag it down even further.

Please, do the opposite of every bone-headed thing you have read. Drag the world up to your level. Don't let the douchebags win. While they're always desperately trying to drag the bar of society down, do us all a favour and drag it right back up again. Fight the douchebag, don't join him.

CHAPTER 26

COP OUT (OF HIS MIND)

IT WAS A QUIET Sunday morning in early autumn. The sky was overcast and the air was frigid. I was on the road early that morning, on my way to attend a motorcycle maintenance course.

I was driving my pickup truck and I was, more or less, the only vehicle on the road. The streets were sleepy, as was I. Judging by the number of cars on the road, everyone but me was still in bed. It didn't matter to me though, because I was looking forward to getting my hands dirty.

Driving down a long stretch of road that I had all to myself, another vehicle suddenly appeared in my rear-view mirror. It was closing in on me fast. It didn't matter. It was a four lane road, so the dude could pass me by in the adjacent lane without a problem.

I stayed the course and took in some of the scenery as I drove in the right hand. It's not often that you get to drive without many other cars around. There was a nice patch of evergreen forest to my right, and because the road was so empty, I could appreciate its beauty. I was driving a touch over the speed limit, but nothing too crazy. I wasn't in a rush so I didn't need to put the pedal down too far.

Before I knew it, the guy driving behind me had closed the distance. Instead passing me by in the other lane, he chose to drive right on my ass. Shit, he was nearly up my ass. I didn't know what the hell his problem was, because there was a completely unobstructed lane to the left of us that he could have changed into at any point in order to pass me. But he never did.

The nut job was driving a dark blue GMC Suburban that was covered in mud from roof to running boards. I don't like anyone tailgating me, and when it's a truck that's bigger than mine, it pisses me off even further. Was I to get rear-ended in my Dodge Dakota by something like a little Mini, it would not cause near the damage to my person as would being rear-ended by a large Suburban.

Needless to say, my mood was changing. I was no longer taking in the scenery.

I was wondering what the hell this guy's deal was. Was he too retarded to realize that there was another, unobstructed lane directly beside him? Was he still pissed-drunk from one hell of a Saturday night bender, unable to see the lines clearly enough to know he could safely pass? I didn't know and I didn't care. I was not pleased.

I decided that if he wasn't going to make use of the lane to the left of us, I would. So, I changed into it in order to get the dip shit off my ass.

I was now giving him ample opportunity to pass me in the lane in which he was travelling. All he had to do was step on it. He didn't even have to change lanes.

To my surprise, he did not take the opportunity I presented him with. As I was now out of his way, I thought he would stay the course in the unobstructed lane and go blow right past me. He did not.

He, instead, changed lanes, pulling his Suburban directly in behind me once again. He was up my ass so far that had I a hemorrhoid, it would have been jealous. As if his behaviour wasn't strange enough to begin with, it was now simply fucked up.

There were still no other cars but the two of us on that stretch of road. For some reason, the asshole behind me must have wanted our two vehicles become one. His filthy Suburban was trying to make my Dakota its bitch, and my Dakota wasn't too happy at all about it. She didn't want any tap ass.

I was perplexed. I didn't know what the hell was going on. In all my years on the road, no one had ever done something that strange to me before. Sure, there are an absolute abundance of morons on the road who I've witnessed doing all sorts of strange manoeuvres over the years, but this guy took the cake.

Irritated and confused, I decided to change lanes once again. I pulled my truck back into the right hand lane and, I shit you not, the fucker behind me did the exact same thing a moment after I did. I couldn't believe it! He had now followed me through two separate lane changes and was still tailgating my truck.

By this point, I was starting to wonder if I had some sort of deranged lunatic operating the truck behind me. Maybe he had just escaped from the insane asylum and had stolen the first vehicle he had stumbled across? Maybe he was a psychopathic serial killer? To be honest, I didn't really know what to think. I was worried that this asshole was going to cause a completely unnecessary smash-up.

At that moment, I wished that I could have been driving somewhere like Arizona, so that I could legally have had a gun in my glove compartment. If anyone has ever deserved to have a tire shot out on his vehicle, it was the extreme douchebag behind me. But I didn't have a gun. Damn gun legislation!

I decided, at that point, to step on it a little. I wanted to put a bit of distance between the two of us, and clearly changing lanes twice didn't help me achieve that outcome. I wanted to extricate that Suburban pimple from my ass, and clearly nothing short of speeding up would achieve that result. It was my only option at the moment.

So, I accelerated. I was approaching an intersection and I wondered if I were to pull off on the approaching road if the deranged asshole behind me would do the same. I had no idea as to what were his intentions. Maybe he didn't either. But I was mad, so I was hoping that he would pull over behind me because, by that point, I really wanted to kick the piss out of the motherfucker. I don't take lightly to someone going out of their way to cause a high speed car accident with me. I value my life, even if he doesn't value his.

But it was not to be. Before I could pull over, something very surprising happened. From out of the Suburban, mere feet behind me, came an array of flashing blue and red lights. He was a cop!

I was shocked. I couldn't believe it. This whole time it had been a cop erratically driving behind me. Or was it? Did someone steal an unmarked cop cruiser and decide to fuck with me? That seemed unlikely.

So there I was thinking I had a road-raging degenerate, psychopath tailgating me through lane changes, when the whole time it had been a road-raging, degenerate psychopathic cop tailgating me through lane changes.

My anger grew exponentially. When I thought it was just some lunatic behind me, I was pissed off. But now that I knew it was a lunatic cop behind me, I was ready to rumble. Don't you come barking up my tree and looking for trouble.

I wanted nothing more than to feed the whack job a knuckle sandwich or two. This dude had endangered my life for absolutely no reason. The bastard had tried to give me a Suburban enema. I felt it unfair that he was a cop.

First off all, he had a gun, so it was already an unfair fight. I'd have to take him out before he could reach for the pistol. Secondly, if I did what it was that I truly wanted to do – what he truly deserved - and I beat him within a breath of his life, I'd probably go to jail because he had a badge. That made me even more irritated!

A block or two down the road I pulled over. The cop pulled in behind me. To my surprise, he came to a stop about twenty feet back from my vehicle. That was roughly nineteen feet further from my bumper than he had previously been when we were driving. Even though I was fuming mad, I didn't show it. I appeared calm, cool and collected.

After literally sitting there for an entire minute, the douchebag finally decided to step down and out of his vehicle. And boy, was it ever a step down. The cop couldn't have been any taller than five foot three.

Now, I'm by no means a tall man, but I definitely had some significant height on this guy. It looked comical to see this little guy getting out of the driver's side of such a big vehicle. He almost needed a step stool to dismount.

I suppose, because of the way he was driving, I was expecting a much larger and more menacing-looking man. I had envisioned a very large and aggressive freak, covered in tattoos and army fatigues. What I had on my hands, instead, was a small, red-headed cop with a serious case of Little Man Syndrome. He looked like an angry little leprechaun.

Cops can be assholes. Woman cops can be even worse. But the worst cop of all, by far, is a small man who is insecure about his size, or lack thereof.

A guy with Little Man Syndrome is the worst possible person to put in a position of authority. Giving a loaded gun and a badge to a sufferer of such a disorder is kind of like strapping a hair triggered pistol to an irate Chihuahua that just snorted a dusting of cocaine from the coffee table of a Columbian drug lord. What I'm saying is that it's not a good idea.

As the douchebag cop approached, I could see by his reflection in my side mirror that he meant business. Clad in a solid blue uniform with black-laced boots, the little ginger's face could not have possessed a more serious look.

Even though I was angry, the excessive ferocity on the idiot's face brought a smile to mine. It was comical. I didn't know what his problem was or why he was trying so hard to look so intensely serious. Hell, I didn't even know what I had been pulled over for. As far as I was concerned, all I was guilty of was trying to avoid a lunatic in a mud-caked SUV. I was being fucked with.

I waited until the cop was standing still beside my truck door before I slowly rolled down the window. He had made me wait far too long for him to get out of his truck and saunter over to me. I figured the least I could do was to make him wait for me to slowly roll down my window. Tit for tat, you little bastard. Tit for tat.

Once I had finally rolled down my window at a painstakingly slow pace, the little douchebag demanded, in a very serious tone, to see my license and registration. I obliged without saying a word. I was very curious to see where he was going to take this encounter.

After taking a brief look at my documents, the man asked me if I knew why I had been pulled over. I did not, and that is what I told him. Based on his immediate reaction, my response was not the one he wanted to hear.

The angry cop started to berate me, right then and there. I couldn't believe it. He was freaking out, losing his mind, hollering at me as if I had just killed a child in the street with my truck and then fled the scene while dragging the little corpse behind. The moron was excessively over-reacting to the fact that I had done nothing wrong. If only a lightning bolt could have struck him dead right then and there, justice would have been served.

According to the psycho, I had been in the wrong. That was news to me but I let him continue. He told me that he had been following me for blocks and that he had witnessed me as I took my truck from a position of speeding to a position of excessive speeding. Actually, he didn't so much tell it to me as he did scream it at me. This reject from hell was clearly upset. I couldn't believe it. I felt like I was being punked. I was waiting for a television host to appear from behind a hidden camera. That never happened.

I decided that my best plan of attack would be to remain calm through the berating. I let the douchebag holler at me for what must have been a solid minute before I spoke. The last thing he said to me before I broke my silence was to tell me that I had been excessively speeding through a 50 km/h zone. I finally opened my mouth to interject and inform him that it was a 60 km/h zone we had been driving through.

He did not appreciate my candour. As a result, he resumed hollering, screaming that I was wrong, that it was indeed a 50 km/h zone. The mental case would not calm down or stop yelling. He was like a two year old child in a full blown temper tantrum. He had, long ago, gone well past the point mere inappropriateness. He was now getting to the point where I thought that I was actually going to have to get out of my truck and have a fist fight with a cop, right in the middle of the street.

Had he not been an officer of the law, I would have beaten severely. Nobody has the right to speak to anyone in the manner with which he addressed me, especially after what he had done to me. However, due to the fact that he had a badge, a gun, and that there was probably a video camera pointed at me from inside of his vehicle, I refrained.

Instead, I waited until he ran out of breath. Eventually, I suppose he exhausted himself because he finally had to take a breath in. When he did, I asked him, calmly, if he was finally done. He glared at me in response and sternly told me to stay put while he went back to his truck to write me up a ticket.

'I don't think so' I said to him. 'What are you going to write me a ticket for, anyway? Trying to evade a road-raging maniac? Is it now illegal to try to protect oneself from imminent harm?'

He looked at me with a confused look on his face. All he could muster in response was the word, 'What?'

So I asked him why he was wasting his time writing me a ticket, when in reality he should be writing himself a ticket and cutting up his own licence on the spot. I asked him if it was normal behaviour for a cop to randomly decide to tailgate a civilian driver who was minding his own business.

Then I asked him why he would do such a dangerous thing. I told him that I thought his job was to make the streets safer, not more dangerous. I also mentioned, again, that he was wrong about the posted speed limits, and if he liked, he could take a drive back in the direction from which we came to see that he was wrong.

It was like I had caught him with a sucker punch. I had taken all the wind out of his lungs. Since he finally appeared to have nothing to say, I decided to keep on going. If I couldn't hit him with my fists, I could at least hit him with my words. I wasn't about to let him off the hook that easily. I wanted to see the crazy wee bastard squirm.

'Am I a victim of some sort of strange police entrapment? I wasn't speeding. I was just driving along minding my own business, when out of the blue, you and your filthy Suburban flew up onto my ass. You appeared to have absolutely no intention of going around me, so I graciously changed lanes to allow you easy passage. Instead of continuing on your way, you decided to change lanes in behind me and to continue to tailgate me. Dumbfounded, I changed lanes once again to try to shake you from my ass, but it didn't work because you switched lanes in behind me yet again. At this point I thought I had a full-fledged lunatic on my ass. Actually, it would appear as if I was right. You are a full-fledged lunatic. Therefore, I had no choice but to speed up in order to put a little bit of distance between us, and it was at that moment that you turned your red and blue's on. It would appear to me that you did everything in your power to force me to speed. That would seem to be unethical, wouldn't you agree? Did your boss tell you this morning that you were a little light on speeding tickets for the month? A man like you should not have a badge.'

Before I could continue on any further, the massive douchebag handed me back my license and told me, in a calm and quite voice, to have a good day. He then walked back to his truck, got in, and sped away.

I couldn't believe what had just transpired. Had I not stood up for myself in that messed up situation, that asshole cop would have bent me over and raped me with speeding tickets, and Lord knows what else?

He was a demented little leprechaun who should never have been allowed to become a police officer. Who knows how many other people that little coward's done shit like that to? He's probably broken down a lot of people and sent a lot of women into uncontrollable fits of crying. I probably should have kicked his ass, cop or not.

When all was said and done, I was pissed off at myself for not getting his name badge number. I should have reported his demented behaviour to the cop shop. But at least I had a bit of a moral victory. I sent him off with his tail between his legs and for that I was pleased.

Bar none, he was the biggest douchebag cop I have ever encountered, and I've encountered a few. I wonder how he gets on with his co-workers? Perhaps one day he will be caught in a fire-fight and will succumb to 'friendly fire'. If only the world were that fair a place.

CONCLUSION

HOLD BACK those tears. Sadly, we have come to an end. I hope this book has enlightened you in a way that no other has done before. May I pray that it has provided you with knowledge and insight that, until now, was found only inside of my twisted and juvenile mind. If you're ever in doubt of how to conduct yourself in any of life's situations, doing the opposite of all the douchebag behaviours I have written about is probably a good place to start.

At this point in time I would like to apologize for any injuries to your stomach muscles that may have incurred as a result of the endless fits of laughter that this masterwork has provided. It is not my fault that I am as witty and funny as I am humble. Now your wounds may finally begin to heal. Perhaps you should go out and get yourself a book from Oprah's book club to aid with your recovery. Her favourite books will heal you physically, mentally and spiritually. Or they just might make you vomit profusely, adding further injury to your already strained abdomen. On second thought, maybe hold off on the Oprah's book club readings for the time being.

While some of you may have laughed your way through the book, perhaps others were angered or offended by the filth and garbage I have spewed throughout this work of literary genius. Perhaps you couldn't be happier that it's over. Your anger can finally subside and your unnaturally high blood pressure can, once again, return to non-life-threatening levels.

But to be serious for just a moment, I enjoyed writing all these mindless rants and anecdotes and I hope that you enjoyed reading them. It was cathartic. This book got a lot off my chest. And if you were honestly offended by anything I wrote, you are a douchebag, but thanks for reading.

If you take anything from this book let it be this – don't be a douchebag. I hate douchebags and there are an awful lot of them out there. So do your part to help out by spreading the message of this book far and wide. The single greatest thing you can do for society is to get everyone you encounter to buy their very own copy of this book. Spread the word. The world is counting on you. Don't let it down!

The main text of this book is set in BEMBO, a typeface family designed by Stanley Morison in 1929. It was based on a typeface designed by Francesco Griffo, who worked as a punch-cutter for famed early printer and publisher Aldus Manutius in Venice. The typeface was first used in February 1496, in the setting of a 60 page text written by the young Italian humanist poet Pietro Bembo, later a Cardinal and secretary to Pope Leo x.

The title page is set in **CHAMPION GOTHIC MIDDLEWEIGHT**, a typeface family designed by Jonathan Hoefler in 1990. Originally developed for *Sports Illustrated*, the Champion Gothic series was created to help designers deal with headlines of different lengths. American woodtypes of the late nineteenth century served as the inspiration for Champion Gothic, in both form and philosophy.

Perhaps the greatest book of poetry ever written. Matthew James is a sheer genius and a cunning linguist. He paints words onto a page the way da Vinci did onto ceilings, or was that Michelangelo? Either way, he's impressive. The emotionality of this master work explodes from the pages and hits you straight in the face with a walloping force.

This book will mesmerize and provocatize. Nothing is taboo to Matthew James. He regularly breaks boundaries with his insights on subjects like sex, liquor fuelled promiscuity, and women. Considered by the Incas to be a cross between William Shakespeare and Wilt Chamberlain, Matthew James is truly a genius of our time. Please, let him put his poems in you. They won't disappoint.

WWW.ENGAGEBOOKS.CA

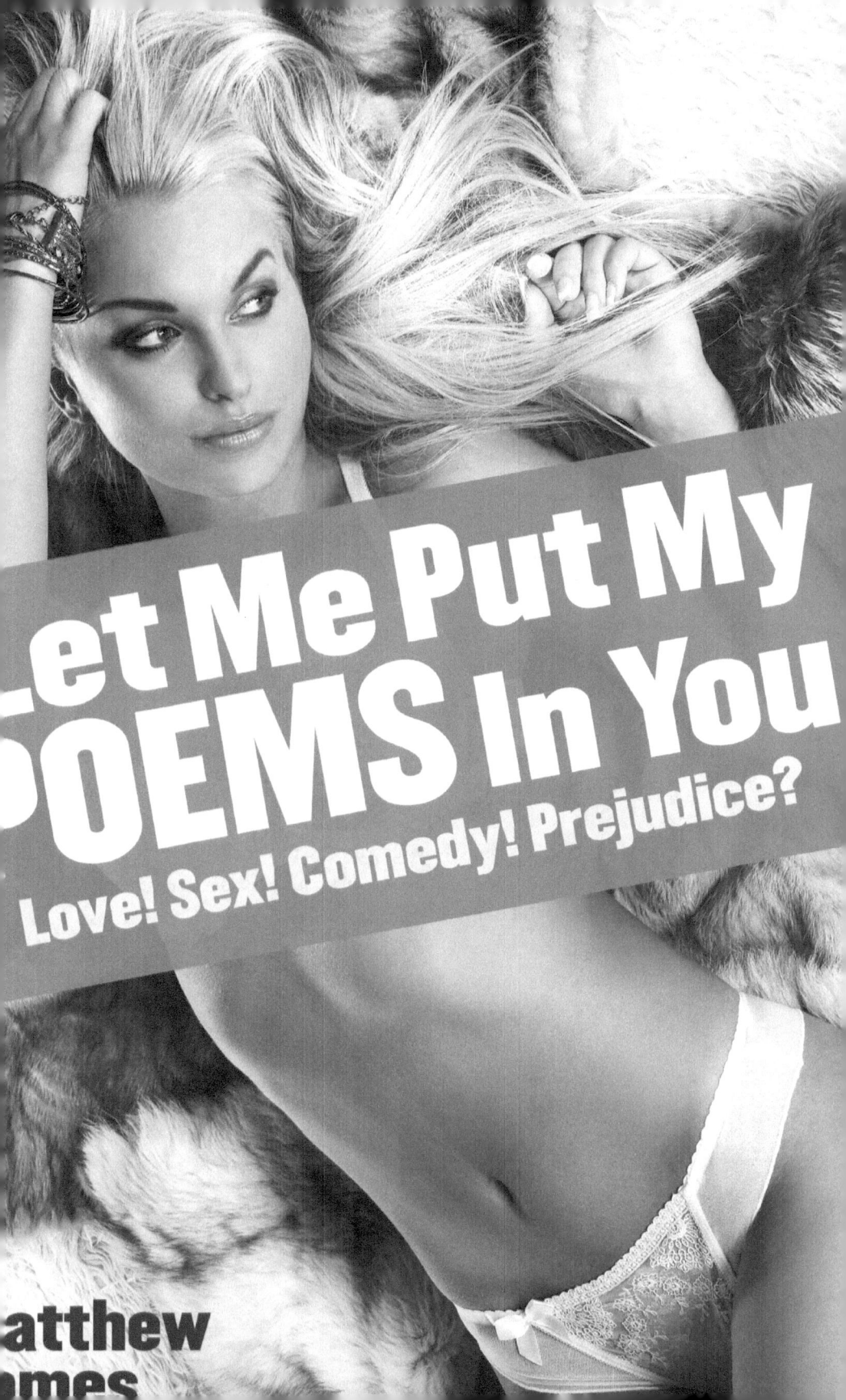

Let Me Put My POEMS In You

Love! Sex! Comedy! Prejudice?

matthew
ames

That's right, America! You never asked for it and you were heard, loud and clear. Matthew James is a man possessed. You can sleep with one eye open. You can sleep with the other one open too. But it won't matter because nothing is going to prevent Matthew James from becoming the next president of the United States of America.

With rugged good looks, an IQ that is boldly average and a Canadian passport, Matthew James is more than equipped to lead the American people wherever they need to be lead. His platforms on such topics as war, the economy and national security will revolutionize the world, and when Matthew speaks of the world, he means America.

Matthew James is a man of the people. Matthew James is a man who is people. Matthew James is a leader of the people. Matthew James will, in 2016, be the commander in chief of the American people.

His political manifesto will gently assault your soul. Read it, fall in love with it, and fall in love with your next president, America. This political manifesto will change your life, perhaps even for the better. Do yourself the best thing you've ever done in the past minute of your life and read this book. America! America! America?

WWW.ENGAGEBOOKS.CA

www.ingramcontent.com/pod-product-compliance
Lightning Source LLC
Chambersburg PA
CBHW050940120626
46552CB00001B/297